**"You have to be th** ❏ **ever met.**

"After I just about bit your head off, too."

"I hate to break this to you, darlin'," he said with a laugh, "but you don't scare me."

Once seated, they both spread out their lunches on the blanket to share.

"Sure beats eating in the back room with the crew."

"Do you mean the food or the company?"

Looking over at her, he grinned. "Both."

"Flattery will get you nowhere with me, country boy," she warned, though the sudden blush on her cheeks said otherwise. "But you get an A for effort."

"Just callin' it like I see it."

That made her laugh. "The girls around here must fall all over themselves trying to get your attention."

"Nah. I'm just Heath, the goofball they all grew up with."

"That's not what I've heard," she informed him.

"That was a long time ago. Now I'm looking for a wife who thinks I hung the moon, and a bunch of kids who think I'm the greatest dad ever."

"Really?" Tess asked incredulously. "That's all?"

"To me, that's everything."

**Mia Ross** loves great stories. She enjoys reading about fascinating people, long-ago times and exotic places. But only for a little while, because her reality is pretty sweet. Married to her college sweetheart, she's the proud mom of two amazing kids, whose schedules keep her hopping. Busy as she is, she can't imagine trading her life for anyone else's—and she has a pretty good imagination. You can visit her online at miaross.com.

## Books by Mia Ross

### Love Inspired

### *Barrett's Mill*

*Blue Ridge Reunion*
*Sugar Plum Season*
*Finding His Way Home*
*Loving the Country Boy*

### *Holiday Harbor*

*Rocky Coast Romance*
*Jingle Bell Romance*
*Seaside Romance*

*Hometown Family*
*Circle of Family*
*A Gift of Family*
*A Place for Family*

Visit the Author Profile page at Harlequin.com for more titles.

# Loving the
# Country Boy

## Mia Ross

HARLEQUIN® LOVE INSPIRED®

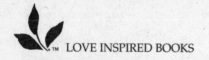 

LOVE INSPIRED BOOKS

Recycling programs
for this product may
not exist in your area.

ISBN-13: 978-0-373-81855-6

Loving the Country Boy

www.Harlequin.com

**Printed in U.S.A.**

And over all these virtues put on love, which binds them all together in perfect unity.
—*Colossians* 3:14

For Rob

## Acknowledgments

To the very talented folks who help me
make my books everything they can be:
Elaine Spencer, Melissa Endlich and
the dedicated staff at Love Inspired.

As always, huge thanks to the gang at
Seekerville (seekerville.net). It's a great place
to hang out with readers—and writers!

I've been blessed with a wonderful network of
supportive, encouraging family and friends.
You inspire me every day!

# *Chapter One*

Tess Barrett was not a morning person.

Of course, that might have had something to do with the fact that her California-girl brain hadn't quite adjusted to Virginia time yet. Or maybe it was the dark blue sedan she'd borrowed from her grandmother, a far cry from the jazzy red convertible she'd left in LA. Yawning, she looked around and couldn't help admiring the lush scenery on the other side of the windshield. Ordinarily, she drove to work through bumper-to-bumper traffic jams, with the AC on full blast and palm trees waving at her as she passed by.

On this cool October morning, hers was the only car in sight on a gravel road that wasn't even two lanes wide. Towering oak and maple trees stood alongside the lane like guards, their branches arching overhead to form a tunnel of leaves ranging in color from pale green to gold to brilliant red. When the early sunlight started peeking through the canopy, it lit the whole area in a breathtaking display that would be right at home on an artist's easel.

Normally she wasn't the poetic type, and her creative impression of her surroundings startled her, to say the least. She must be more tired than she realized. Or, she thought as she drove around a curve in the unfamiliar back-country road, her fuzzy brain just needed caffeine.

Fortunately, she had some of her grandmother's secret blend of coffee mixed with cream and berries. Reaching toward the cup holder, she glanced down to grasp the handle of her stainless-steel travel mug. Just as she was lifting it free, the sound of a blaring horn jerked her eyes back to the road. Letting go of the cup, she cranked the steering wheel to the right and slammed on the brakes in a terrifying hailstorm of dust and gravel.

She swallowed hard to get her heart out of her throat and sat very still, taking stock of everything. She was unharmed, and the car was in one piece, although it sat cocked at an unnatural angle on the verge of the ditch. Framed in her driver's window was an antique delivery truck that had quite possibly been one of the first ones put into service. Sporting as much rust as metal, one thing about it stood out as new. Someone had gone to the trouble to freshen up the logo on the driver's door.

*Barrett's Sawmill, Barrett's Mill, Virginia.*

Her eyes traveled upward to find the driver staring through his open window at her. With his shock of sun-bleached blond hair and deep blue eyes, she recognized him instantly. "Heath Weatherby?"

His tanned face split into a wide grin. "So, you remember me?"

"Sure, I do."

Vividly. At her cousin Scott's wedding last month, she'd watched Heath flirt his way through all the single women at the reception. He'd brought to mind a lion stalking a herd of gazelle, hunting for one he could easily bring down. She'd had her fill of guys like that, so his very obvious technique hadn't left her with the best impression of him. Still, he was Scott's friend, so she plastered on the friendly customer-service smile she'd cultivated in the boutique where she worked.

*Used to work*, she corrected herself with a mental sigh. Yet another in a long line of failures she'd managed to accumulate in twenty-eight years, that position was history. Tess currently had no clue what lay ahead of her, but being late for her new job wasn't how she wanted to start.

Heath clambered out of the old truck, and she expected him to start yammering about how she should have been watching the road more carefully. Instead, he rested his hands on the roof of the car and leaned in to stare at her with obvious concern. "You okay?"

"A little shaken up, but basically I'm fine." Those eyes were studying her way too closely, and she turned away to retrieve her purse from the spot on the floor where it had landed after their near-impact. "Do you want my insurance card?"

For some crazy reason, he started laughing. Irked by his blasé attitude, she glared up at him. "Did I say something funny?"

"We didn't hit each other or anything, and even if we had there'd be no need to drag an adjuster all the way out here. I work on your gram's car all the time, so I'll fix whatever's wrong."

"That's nice of you, but I heard a pretty loud crunching sound. The parts could get expensive, and I don't want to pay for it." She left out the part about not having the money to cover much of a car repair bill. That would sound pathetic, and since she hadn't confided her money problems to Gram, she wasn't about to share them with a stranger. Not even a great-looking one wearing a you-can-count-on-me grin.

"Wasn't planning to charge you for it."

She wasn't sure what to make of that. In her experience, whenever someone suggested something outside the norm, the situation turned out badly. For her. "I don't know."

"Why don't we have a look, and then we'll decide?"

Her foggy, sleep-deprived brain couldn't come up with a decent protest, so she simply nodded. Heath opened the door for her and stood back to give her room to step out. Logically, she knew it wasn't possible, but she thought he was taller than he'd been when they'd first met. Dressed in worn jeans and a denim shirt with *Morgan's Garage* and his name stitched over the pocket, he had the solid, dependable look of a man who could live up to his promise to fix things that were broken. And not just cars.

That dreamy impression flitted through her mind before she could stop it, and she firmly clamped down before any more had a chance to follow it. With a string of bad relationships to her credit, she'd promised herself that for the foreseeable future, she'd keep her life clear of male distractions. Despite having every possible advantage, she'd accomplished nothing of value beyond earning a bachelor's degree and holding a series of retail positions whose main attraction was the employee discount.

If that was going to change, she recognized that she'd have to figure out how to make it happen. For herself, and by herself. Not like her mother, who was still struggling to recover from a ninja-style divorce that had stripped her of her glittering lifestyle and a good chunk of her pride. Tess knew that if she wanted her own story to end differently, it was time for her to take control of her life and find a way to make it work. Her own failed engagement had finally convinced her that relying too heavily on someone else simply wasn't worth the risk.

The sound of Heath's boots crunching in the gravel brought her back to the problem at hand, and she dutifully trailed after him. Hunkering down, he ducked his head under the front end of the sedan for a better look. She was no expert, but any moron could figure out the car wouldn't roll with that wad of crumpled metal wrapped around the right front tire.

"That doesn't look good." What a stupid thing to say, she chided herself, and waited for him to pile on with some criticism of his own. She was well accustomed to that, and she braced herself for the shot.

Instead, he glanced up at her with the kind of amused look he might have used with a curious child. "Yeah, I was thinking the same thing."

"I wasn't trying to be funny."

"I don't doubt it." He started to say something else but apparently thought better of it and focused back on the damaged pieces.

Her reflexive response was to demand what he meant by that, but she managed to stop herself. It was too early in the day for a battle of wills, and considering how her morning had gone so far, she'd probably come out on the losing end. Besides, he was clearly going out of his way to help her, and she didn't want him to think she was ungrateful. So she swallowed her sharp words and asked, "Will it be hard to fix?"

"Nah. Couple days, tops." Standing, he brushed his hands off and rested them on his hips. "Like I said, I'll take care of it, no charge."

She was sorely tempted to take him up on his offer. A month ago, she'd have accepted without a second thought, allowing someone else to step in and make her life easier. But in the interest of taking responsibility for herself, she didn't feel right about doing that anymore.

"I can't let you do that," she countered in a

firm but polite voice. "It's not your fault I was paying more attention to the scenery than the road."

"Yeah, I could see how that'd happen. It's real pretty out here."

Male admiration twinkled in his eyes, and she narrowed her own in disgust. "Let's get one thing straight right now, country boy."

"Okay."

The casual way he said it made it clear her warning had no impact on him at all. Unlike other guys, who backed up a step when she blasted them with her don't-mess-with-me glare. At five-three, she didn't physically intimidate anyone over the age of ten, so that look was her only option when she wanted to make a point. Either he was braver than most people she knew, or more foolish. Whatever the case, she wasn't thrilled to lose the one advantage she'd ever been able to cultivate.

Summoning her iciest tone, she said, "I'm here to help out at the mill while Chelsea's on maternity leave. Period, end of story. Whatever you're selling, I'm not buying. Got it?"

"Got it." Punctuating his reply with a quick nod, he moved out to a more respectable distance. "Can I ask you a question, though?"

"Sure."

"What's with the attitude? All I did was give

you a compliment, and you act like I'm trying to work you over."

"In my experience, when a man tells a woman how pretty she is, he's expecting it to get him somewhere."

"Well, now, don't I feel silly?" Heath drawled with a mischievous grin. "I was just lookin' for a smile."

Despite her best efforts to control it, she felt one tugging at the corner of her mouth, threatening to upend her disapproving frown. After a few seconds, she gave in and let it come through. Unfortunately, that seemed to encourage him, and his face broke into a victorious grin. "There it is. That wasn't so hard, was it?"

Tess opened her mouth for a sharp retort then decided there was no point. She had reacted to him as if he was a leering stranger on the street. When she replayed her stern warning in her head, she felt her face heating with embarrassment. He might be a little too suave for her liking, but Heath wasn't dangerous.

"No, it wasn't." Realizing that wasn't enough, she went on. "I apologize for being so rude. I guess I'm still wiped out from my trip, and for a West Coast girl like me it's four o'clock in the morning."

"Yeah, that trip east is a real killer. I worked

in Alaska for a while, and it took me a week to recover from the flight home."

"What did you do in Alaska?" she blurted before remembering that she was late for work and should keep their conversation short and sweet. Then again, a few more minutes probably wouldn't make much difference one way or the other. "I've never been there, but from all the Travel Channel shows I've watched, it looks like a fascinating place to live."

Sorrow dimmed his bright expression, and his eyes went a murky bluish-gray that could only mean she'd inadvertently struck a nerve. Shortly after they appeared, though, the clouds were gone. "It is. I worked on an oil rig for a couple years and spent a lot of my spare time flying around with my buddy in his bush plane. We ferried tourists and hunters around, and delivered supplies to some villages that actually were in the middle of nowhere."

"It sounds incredible."

"Yeah, it was."

Although his tone was upbeat, it sounded forced to her, as if he were making a concerted attempt to be positive about his Alaskan adventure. Instinct told her something had forced him to return to Barrett's Mill. Something that made him sad, even now. She wouldn't dream of asking him about it, of course, but she couldn't help wondering what had happened to him.

"I'll come back with a wrecker to get Olivia's car," he said, bringing her back to reality. "But in the meantime, I can't just leave you stranded out here. Would you like a ride to the mill?"

That wasn't how she'd intended to begin her new, independent life, but she wasn't exactly dressed for a cross-country hike. "I can call Paul. I don't want you to go out of your way."

"Not out of my way. I was heading there, too, to drop off this truck for Paul."

She looked at him doubtfully. "You were driving in the opposite direction."

"Actually, you were. You must have missed your turn back there. Easy to do."

Her cheeks flushed again, but she stayed silent and just nodded at him, turning toward the car.

While she got her purse, she regretted misjudging the friendly mechanic, lumping him in with the other shallow, manipulative guys she'd known. Not that it mattered, she thought as she followed him over to the truck.

For the time being, she was done with men. With her heart still in pieces, it was safer that way.

\* \* \*

Baffling wasn't the word for Tess Barrett. Sweet one minute, prickly the next, she'd kept him off balance since their bizarre meeting in the middle of the road. Not quite the way he wanted to start his day.

Heath shut the passenger door a little more forcefully than he should have, wincing at the jolt of pain that zipped up his arm to his shoulder. He sometimes forgot it was still healing, and he had to be careful how he moved. The lingering reminder of his past mistakes drove him nuts, but since there was nothing he could do about it, he did his best to shrug it off as he circled the truck and climbed into the cab.

While Heath started the pickup and pulled around the disabled sedan, he couldn't help glancing over at his passenger and wondering what her deal was. He'd grown up running wild with her cousins, the infamous Barrett boys who were the stuff of local legend. Knowing them as well as he did, he definitely pegged the family resemblance in the stunning brunette with the dark, intelligent eyes, sitting beside him.

Other than that, she struck him as a whole different animal. In a slim skirt the color of lilacs and a tissue-thin blouse a couple of shades lighter, she looked decidedly out of place on this backwoods road in the heart of the Blue Ridge valley. Then again, she'd traveled across the country to help out at the iconic sawmill that had given the town its name and still provided many of its residents with a decent income. To do something like that, she must be incredibly generous. Or desperate.

Thinking of her being in trouble bothered him for some reason, so he went with the other option. "It's nice of you to come out and lend a hand with the mill. I'm sure your family really appreciates it."

"At the wedding, Chelsea mentioned she'd be out with the baby for a while and would be looking for someone to take over while she's gone. When I lost my job a couple weeks ago, it seemed like a good time to try something different. So here I am."

"That's great for them but tough for you," he commented with genuine sympathy. "Mind if I ask what happened?"

"Oh, the usual. I was managing an adorable little boutique in Beverly Hills. After a few months, the owner's husband started paying more attention to me than to her, so she fired me."

The sarcastic tone rang a bell with him, and he barely managed to keep back a grin. Apparently, a streak of wry Barrett humor was lurking behind that cool, polished exterior of hers. Interesting.

She didn't volunteer anything more, and Heath took the hint that she'd rather let the subject drop. Fine by him, he mused as he concentrated on the road in front of him. He had enough on his plate these days without taking on someone else's problems.

After a couple of minutes, the silence seemed to get to her. "So, you grew up around here?"

"Born and raised."

"You said you liked Alaska," she pointed out. "Have you been anywhere else?"

"Louisiana, Iowa, Arizona. Being a mechanic, I can pretty much work anywhere."

"What made you decide to come back here?"

Heath still hadn't come to terms with the answer to that, and he fought the urge to joke his way out of responding. He'd been doing that for months, to avoid reliving the pain that had chased him back to the safe, quiet town where he'd spent his childhood. But something told him if he dodged a question from the pretty woman beside him, she'd know it. And she'd never trust him. Why he cared what she thought about him, he couldn't say, but loyalty to her family was as good a reason as any.

As he parked in the turnaround near the mill

house, he finally settled on a version of the truth. "It was time to come home. I'm almost thirty, and my adventuring days are over."

She studied him for a long, uncomfortable moment, and it took everything he had not to look away. Clearly, she suspected that he hadn't given her the whole story, but he hoped his explanation would be enough to satisfy her curiosity, at least for now.

"That's interesting," she said with quiet determination glittering in her eyes. "Because mine are just getting started."

Suddenly, there was a bang in the truck bed behind them, and a big, furry face popped in through the open back window. Tess shrieked and plastered herself up against the passenger door, shielding her head with her designer purse.

Chuckling, Heath greeted their slobbery guest with a pat on the head. "Hey, Boyd. How're you today?"

The bloodhound woofed, licking Heath's hand while his tail wagged enthusiastically. When Heath noticed him eyeballing Tess, he warned, "Behave yourself, dude. The lady's had a tough morning."

In response, the dog sat politely and reeled in his tongue, even though his head was still hanging over the seat. Apparently, that was as good as it was going to get. "Tess, I'd like you to meet Boyd. The story is he found your cousin Paul at a lumber camp in Oregon and followed him home. Personally, I think it was the other way around."

His comment had the intended effect, and she uncoiled herself from the corner to give the hound a cautious once-over. Thrilled with the attention, Boyd let out a quiet woof and cocked his head in what even a committed dog-hater would have called a friendly gesture.

"Pleased to meet you, Boyd," she finally said, patting his forehead. "You'll have to excuse my manners, but you scared me half to death."

The hound woofed again, and Heath reached over to ruffle his floppy ears. "See? He's sorry. He's the welcoming committee around here, and he was just doing his job."

"Very well, too," she added, scratching around his collar with a smile. "Paul found himself a real gem of a sidekick, didn't he?"

Her gooey tone was totally at odds with her hard exterior, and Heath couldn't help admiring how quickly she'd shifted from terrified city girl to down-to-earth animal lover. Apparently, she reserved that cool, distant manner of hers for humans. It probably should have bugged him, but in reality it was a relief.

During the short time they'd spent together, he'd learned that Tess had a sharp mind and a tongue to match. He was fairly well traveled, and experience had taught him to steer clear of women like her. They were always one step ahead of him, and eventually he got tired of trying to catch up.

His conversation with Tess hadn't changed his opinion in the least. In fact, he was determined to give women like Tess a wide berth, now more than ever.

## Chapter Two

After Tess recovered from meeting the very exuberant Boyd, she got out of the truck and took a few moments to absorb her surroundings. A sparkling creek flowed through the nearby woods and under the wide cobblestone bridge that led from the rutted dirt lane to the lumberyard. Once the stream reached the dam and collected in the mill pond, it was ready to be harnessed to power the waterwheel her cousin Paul had restored to grant their ailing grandfather's wish to see the long-shuttered mill up and running again before he died.

Of course, she hadn't known all this before, she groused. Over the weekend, Gram had filled her in on the family history that had been a complete blank for Tess until a month ago. For the hundredth time, she wondered what possible reason her father had for leaving his charming hometown and stubbornly refusing to acknowledge his roots.

Or his own father's death.

Thinking about the grandfather she'd never met still made her misty, especially when she was standing here in the middle of the property he'd cherished so much. She'd learned that it hadn't been easy to keep it in the family, with developers drooling over the acres of untouched woods around the picturesque Sterling Creek. If he'd given in and sold out, he and Gram would have had enough money to travel wherever they wanted to go. Instead, they chose to hold on to the land and live more modestly in this sleepy little town that didn't warrant even a dot on a state map.

"Something wrong?"

Heath's voice broke into her musings, and she glanced over at him. She was about to give her customary "no" when something stopped her, and she frowned. "I'm not sure. I was just thinking about how my grandfather never wanted to give this place up, even when people offered him a ton of money for it. My father always thought Granddad was crazy."

"Sounds like you agreed with him."

"I know it sounds disrespectful, but yes, I did."

Heath rested an arm over the railing on the

front porch steps and cocked his head with a curious look. "And now?"

"I think I get it, at least a little."

As the breeze rustled through a nearby stand of trees, she admired the spectrum of colors waving along the branches and caught the flash of a white tail as a deer bounded back into the woods. Add in the chiming of dozens of birds and the telltale scent of wood shavings, and her appreciation for the Barrett legacy deepened. Peaceful but teeming with life, this place was a lot more than a chunk of prime real estate. And it was infinitely more valuable than even her brilliant father could possibly fathom.

"I'm sorry you didn't get to meet Will," Heath said gently, as if he'd picked up on her melancholy train of thought. "He was one of the kindest, most generous people I've ever known."

She knew Heath meant for her to view the comment in a positive light, but it only made her choke up again. Pulling herself together wasn't easy, but for both their sakes she dredged up a halfhearted smile. "I don't know what's wrong with me. I was fine at the cemetery with Gram yesterday."

"That's 'cause he's not there. He's here." Heath nodded in the general direction of the rushing water.

The rugged mechanic didn't strike her as the philosophical type, and she eyed him with curiosity. "You really believe that, don't you?"

"Sure. I know it's not a big, exciting city, but for most of us, this little swath of land beats them all, hands down."

He said it without hesitation, but something flickering in his eyes made her suspect that for him, there was more to it than mere loyalty. Since neither of them had the time for a story right now, she opted to let it go. "Since you said you were dropping off that old truck, I'm guessing you need a ride back into town. Did you want to come in and say hello or get going now?"

"No hurry," he replied with a grin. "This is Barrett's Mill, remember?"

Yes, it was. She still wasn't sure what that meant exactly, but she was looking forward to finding out. She and Heath climbed the steps together, with Boyd lumbering up behind them. When Heath pulled open the door, the dog eyed the lobby then turned his large brown eyes on Tess as if he were waiting for her.

"What nice manners you have," she cooed, patting his head on her way past. Paul was standing inside, and she teased, "Did you teach him to do that?"

"Yeah, right," he laughed before hugging her. "So, whattya think of the old place?"

"It looks fabulous, just like you described it." The praise came easily, because even a totally non-mechanical person like her could tell how much effort had gone into bringing the archaic family business back to life.

"Thanks." Shaking hands with Heath, Paul added, "How's the old beast running these days?"

"Are you kidding me?" Heath growled, although the proud twinkle in his eyes gave him away. "She makes a Swiss watch look like a clunker."

"That's great, 'cause the lease just ran out on one of our trucks, and we could use another delivery vehicle around here."

What he wasn't saying, Tess noticed, was that he hadn't renewed the lease. Which meant finances weren't in the best shape right now. Maybe she could do something about that, she thought, relishing the idea of using her college education for something more worthwhile than catering to wealthy customers. She couldn't imagine anything fitting that bill better than pitching in to help improve the mill's bottom line.

For now, though, she needed a way to get herself to and from work. "Speaking of vehicles…"

"Don't tell me," Paul groaned.

"It was an accident. Gram and I were up late, and I couldn't find the bag with my shoes, and—"

"I sort of cut her off turning onto Mill Road," Heath interrupted with a sheepish look that would have convinced the most jaded Hollywood director to hire him on the spot. "The damage isn't bad, and I'll have it fixed in a couple days, tops. For free, since it was my fault."

Even though he'd told her the same thing earlier, Tess still couldn't believe he was so blithely taking responsibility for their run-in. She was trying to figure out why when a soft voice asked, "Are you all right?"

Tess glanced over and saw Paul's wife, Chelsea, silhouetted in the hallway that separated the front end of the mill house from the saws on the production floor. Wearing a burgundy dress with a high-waisted tie, she slowly waddled over to join them.

Not wanting to worry her very pregnant boss, Tess forced a smile and stepped forward for a reassuring hug. "Just embarrassed to be late for my first day of work. How are you?"

"Fine. I wanted to be up front when you got here, but the baby's been pounding on some uncomfortable places this morning."

Tess caught Paul's concerned scowl and studied his wife more closely. While she was clearly trying to hide it, she appeared to be far past exhausted. Beyond that, the way she was standing betrayed the fact that she was actually in pain.

"Chelsea," Paul began in a gentle voice, "I think you should sit down."

"I've been sitting down," she snapped in frustration. "I took a walk, I lay down on that old settee in the store room. Nothing I do makes any difference, so I'm going to stand."

Obviously accustomed to a hormonal mood swing or two, he didn't respond but met her stormy look head-on. She glared at him for a moment before relenting with a frustrated sigh. "I'm sorry, everyone. I'm just having a bad morning."

"It's not the first one," Paul pointed out. "I'm glad we're seeing the doctor today."

"Our appointment's at one," she said to Tess. "I hate to leave you alone so soon, but you can call me if you have any questions."

"Not a problem at all," Tess assured her warmly. Looking around, she noted the feminine touches in the waiting area, from the gingham cushions to the curtains waving in the breeze. Admiring the framed photos of the mill from its Civil War beginnings to the present day, she turned to Chelsea. "Everything looks great. You've done an amazing job in here."

"You should check out the saws," Heath piped up enthusiastically. "It's awesome to see them when they're all running."

While she appreciated his enthusiasm, she couldn't shake the feeling that there was more to his boyish reaction than simple nostalgia. In deference to her sanity, she didn't normally dwell on her less than stellar past. But Heath's fondness for his made her wish she held that kind of affection for the life she'd been living.

Pushing her brooding aside, she shifted her focus to Paul. "At the wedding, Chelsea told me your dad converted the equipment to run on electricity years ago. What made you decide to go back to water power?"

"Waterwheels are cool," the two guys said in unison, making her and Chelsea laugh.

"Well, I can't argue with that," Tess allowed. "Do you have time to show me now?"

He grinned proudly. "I'm between runs, so come on in."

Giving in to her fatigue, Chelsea waved them along. "Daisy and I will be in the office when you're done."

"Your kitty assistant," Tess recalled. "How is she?"

"More trouble than ever, and since she's deaf she can't hear me scolding her. I keep telling myself it's good practice for when I'm chasing after a toddler who won't listen."

As she headed into her office, Tess saw her take a pair of sound-canceling headphones from a hook near the Dutch door. Probably a good idea for herself, too, along with finding a good place to buy more casual clothes and some sensible shoes. This was a far more rustic work environment than she was accustomed to, and she was ridiculously overdressed.

Paul handed her and Heath some shop headphones before donning his own. Then he did a quick visual check of the waterwheel through an opening in the floor and gave them a thumbs-up. With some effort, he pulled a wooden handle that looked to be original to the building and stepped back to join them.

Once everything got up to speed, the entire structure shook as the leather belts whipped around and through the mechanism that ran the huge saws. Used for ripping timber into usable planks, it was hard to believe so much raw power came from damming up one small stream that bubbled so pleasantly through the woods.

When Paul shut everything down, he was

all but humming with excitement for what he'd accomplished. "So?"

"It's amazing. I can't imagine they make most of the parts anymore. Where did you find replacements?"

"Some are still around in one form or another," he explained. "When I could, I modified them to work. When I couldn't, I made 'em myself."

That kind of technical expertise was way beyond her realm of understanding, and she was impressed by his resourcefulness. Not to mention his dogged determination. Resting a hand on his arm, she smiled up at him. "Granddad must've been thrilled when you got this all put back together again."

A bit of the sorrow she felt moved through his eyes, telling her just how much Will Barrett's grandson still missed him. "I'm glad he got to see it."

"So am I."

Heath held the front door open for Tess, admiring her ability to walk in those silly shoes.

"Chelsea, you just put your feet up and relax while I'm gone," Tess ordered as she moved toward the exit. "Make a list of what needs to be done, and you can walk me through it before you and Paul go to the doctor."

"That sounds wonderful, but there's no need to rush back here. Things are pretty quiet right now."

Her claim didn't match up with the job list he'd seen posted in the carpentry area, and Heath gave her a long look. Which she artfully ignored. Once Tess had sidled past him and onto the front porch out of earshot, he leaned his arms on top of the half door and winked at Chelsea. "I know what you're up to, Mrs. Barrett, and you can forget about it."

She blinked at him with all the innocence of a springtime fawn. "What?"

"No need to rush back here." He imitated her musical drawl in a passable falsetto, then switched back to his own voice. "Ya gotta be more subtle if you're planning to take up matchmaking."

"Was it that obvious?" she asked with a laugh. "I thought I was being pretty smooth."

He knew she meant well, so he eased back with a smile. "People get married, start having babies, they get all gooey about stuff like that. I get it, but I don't want you getting any ideas about pairing me up with Tess. I'm not looking for anything serious right now, and she made it clear she's not interested in anything but helping you out while you're on maternity leave."

Brutally clear, he added silently. He didn't

know why her icy warning still stung, but only a complete moron would ignore it.

"She's only been in town a couple of days," Chelsea reminded him. "When she gets more comfortable here, her feelings might change."

"Not hardly," he said evenly. "Besides, she's not staying that long, so there's no point in trying to make something out of nothing."

"But you *would* try, if she wasn't going back to California?"

Heath hesitated. Would he? Their unexpected run-in had knocked him for a loop, and he hadn't quite regained his usually even-keeled perspective. He kept trying to convince himself that was a normal reaction for someone who'd narrowly avoided an accident and was now late for work. The explanation made sense, but part of him knew that wasn't the reason he still felt off-kilter.

It was Tess.

Thinking that way would only get him in trouble, Heath knew, so he shoved the thought back into the corner of his mind he didn't visit very often. "You take care of yourself and that little one. Your assistant will be back soon."

With a good-bye wave, he trotted down the porch steps and met up with Tess just as she was finishing a call. She hit the end button and said, "Gram wanted me to tell you hi and thanks for lending a hand with this."

"Lemme guess," he replied with a grin. "She couldn't care less about the car, and she wants to pay me for the repair work."

"So you're a mind reader," she teased with a mischievous grin that reminded him of her cousins. "What am I thinking?"

The tone was more playful than flirtatious, which was fine with him. Closing his eyes, he rested his fingers on his temples as if he was concentrating very hard. "You're thinking your coffee is cold by now, and you need to get some more while you're in town. Around here, the best place for anything food-related is The Whistlestop."

"Wow," she said around a barely muted yawn, "you're good."

"Not really." He chuckled. "That's the third time you've yawned since we got here. Either you're incredibly bored, or you're not totally awake yet."

He opened the driver's door and motioned for her to get in. When she blinked at him, he realized she wasn't following along. "It's all yours."

"You want me to drive?"

"You're dropping me off, so that's the easiest thing to do." The sunlight glinted off the flecks of gold in her eyes, and he caught a spark of something he couldn't quite put a finger on. But anyone could see he'd hit a nerve with her. "Am I wrong?"

"No, it's just—" She stopped abruptly, and he waited for her to continue. Thankfully, her annoyance drifted away, leaving behind appreciation. "My ex always drove, even if we were in my car and he didn't know where we were going. It kind of bugged me."

"I can see why." He could also understand why the guy was an ex. Anyone that heavy-handed wouldn't last long with this very head-strong woman.

"It's refreshing to be treated like someone with a perfectly good head on her shoulders," she confided with a sigh.

"I can't imagine treating you any other way," Heath blurted before it occurred to him how a comment like that might come across to her. Her grateful smile eased his concern, though, and he was glad he'd spoken his mind.

"Thanks, Heath. That might not seem like much to you, but it means a lot to me."

"You're welcome. Want a hand up?"

"No, I've got it."

Standing on the toe of one high heel, she grasped the interior handle and pulled herself into the cab of the old pickup. He shut the door behind her and strolled around the truck before settling in on the other side. With a little coaching from him, she quickly got the hang of the vintage equipment, and he said, "You're a natural. That clutch isn't the best, but you're doing fine."

"You mean, for a girl?" she teased with a smirk.

Busted, he thought with a grin of his own. Since she didn't seem offended, he figured it wasn't an issue for her. "Sorry, but yeah. The women I've known couldn't handle a brand-new manual transmission, much less this one."

"I guess I'm not like them."

That was an understatement, but he managed not to tell her so. Instead, he pointed out the turn that led to Main Street. With no power steering, the mill truck took some strength to maneuver, and as she made the sharp turn, she groaned with the effort. "This thing handles like a pontoon boat."

Heath chuckled. "Driven a lot of those, have you?"

"Trust me, once was enough."

"Must be a big change, coming here after spending so much time in California."

"Yes, it is."

She didn't offer anything beyond that, but his instincts were telling him it wasn't because she had nothing more to say. They were basically strangers, but he couldn't shake the suspicion that she was holding something back.

None of his business, he cautioned himself as she pulled into the lot at Morgan's Garage and put the truck in Park. All the Barretts were known for their stubborn streak, and despite her upper-class background, Tess seemed to have inherited it in spades. Harsh experience had taught him that the quickest way to irritate a woman was to step in where he wasn't wanted and try to solve a problem she was confident she could handle on her own. Even if she was wrong.

Getting out, he walked over to the driver's window and leaned his elbows on the frame. "If you need anything, you know where to find me."

Her puzzled expression made it clear she had no clue what he was talking about. Then, slowly, understanding dawned in those stunning eyes, and she rewarded him with a grateful smile. "That's sweet of you, but I'm fine. Really," she added emphatically, as if she was trying to convince herself as much as him.

He thought he knew better, but he also knew this wasn't the time to press. Pushing away from the pickup, he said, "Remember this old girl's only got three gears, and her top speed is about forty. Any questions?"

"Actually, I do have one." Angling to face him, she went on. "Why do so many guys refer to cars as female? I mean, women don't call them 'he', so why do you call them 'she'?"

She punctuated her question with an arched brow, and he couldn't help laughing. "I got no idea. Keep her under forty, though, and you should do okay."

"Not a Ferrari." She added a sassy grin. "Got it."

Stepping back, he waved as she left the parking lot and headed for the diner where he'd recommended she get her coffee. This morning had turned out nothing like he'd expected, he mused while he strolled inside to punch in.

With Tess in Barrett's Mill for an extended visit, he had a feeling things around this quiet little town were going to get very interesting.

# Chapter Three

The next morning Tess was pulling her hair into a chignon when her cell phone began playing the ringtone she'd assigned to Chelsea. It was too early in the day for a social call, and she dropped her brush in midstroke to answer it. "Hi, Chelsea. Is everything okay?"

"We had a terrible night, so we're meeting the doctor at his office in half an hour. I'm so sorry to do this to you now. We barely had time to cover anything yesterday."

The stress in her voice came through loud and clear, and she sounded on the verge of tears. The kitchen phone started ringing downstairs, and she assumed it was Paul calling Gram with the same update.

Wishing there was more she could do, Tess summoned a confident tone to reassure her distraught cousin-in-law. "He told you everything was okay at your appointment yesterday, right?"

"Yes."

"I'm sure it'll be the same today. Don't worry about a thing except you and the baby. If I need something, the boys will be there to help me."

"Jason and Scott?" Chelsea scoffed, "They don't even know where we keep the coffee."

"We'll figure it out," Tess promised, hoping she came across as self-assured and reliable. Handling things on her own today was the only option available, so there was no point in considering anything else. "Call when you have some news."

"I will. Thanks so much, Tess. I don't know what we'd do without you."

Because no one had ever viewed her as more than just a pretty face, she'd never gotten that kind of praise in her life. Hearing it now felt incredible, and despite the very grown-up situation she now found herself in, she was smiling when she hung up. Her privileged upbringing had given her plenty of novel adventures through the years, but there was a lot to be said for being in a place where people valued you more for what you could do than how you looked.

When she was ready, she assessed her reflection and was stunned by the enthusiasm lighting the face that stared back at her. Without a drop of makeup, she looked better than she had in months, and she shook her head in amazement. After enjoying herself so much at Scott and Jenna's wedding, she'd expected to appreciate the change of scenery here, but this was something else again.

Buoyed by the energy she felt, she all but skipped down the stairs into the kitchen. Gram was waiting there with a small paper bag and Tess's stainless-steel travel mug, which was giving off the enticing aroma of something exotic. Taking them from her, Tess inhaled and grinned. "This is my favorite blend. Where on earth did you find it around here?"

"Diane brought it by on her way to the teen center earlier," Gram explained. "She picked up a bag of it over in Cambridge for you."

"I'll have to thank Auntie later." Taking a sip, she continued. "I'm assuming that was Paul on the phone a few minutes ago."

Anxiety shadowed her grandmother's eyes, and she nodded. "I've been praying ever since."

"I'm sure they appreciate that."

While Tess wasn't big on religion herself, she knew it brought her grandmother a measure of comfort to feel as if she was doing something constructive rather than just worrying. Then again, if God listened to anyone, it wouldn't surprise her to learn Olivia Barrett had a direct line to heaven.

"Have a good day, dear," Gram said, giving her a quick hug. "If those cousins of yours give you too much trouble, you let me know and I'll set them straight."

Tess laughed, mostly because she knew the Barretts' petite matriarch was only half kidding. "I think Jason and Scott know better than to mess with me, but it's good to know you've got my back."

Waving good-bye, she headed out to where the old mill truck sat in the driveway. Tess was certain Heath had fixed all its annoying idiosyncrasies, so she was totally unconcerned as she buckled herself into the driver's seat and stowed her breakfast before blithely turning the key. Almost as if it was protesting the early hour, the engine began whining but refused to catch.

The sun was beginning to peek over the horizon, and Tess wasn't overjoyed about starting yet another day with car trouble. She couldn't wait to get Gram's stalwart Buick back, she groused silently. It might not be fancy, but it was a large, solid car, and while it wasn't hers, it hadn't given her a bit of trouble.

Unlike that fussy little sports car Avery drove, she thought with a frown.

Born into one of Napa Valley's original vineyard families, at first he'd been enchanted by her undeniable independent streak. *More than just a pretty face*, she could still hear him saying during their engagement party, smiling proudly at the woman he'd chosen to spend the rest of his life with. If she'd known just how short-lived his devotion would be, she would have shoved him into the pool at his family's estate instead of accepting the five-carat diamond ring he'd slipped on her finger.

Water under the bridge, she reminded herself, letting out a frustrated breath to cool her temper. Right now she had to get to work, so she notched the key back in the ignition the way Heath had showed her and tried again. Same result, with an annoying little ping thrown in to test her rapidly fleeting patience.

Someone tapped on the window, and she all but shot through the roof in alarm. When she saw it was Heath, she rested one hand over her racing heart and cranked the window down with the other. "You scared me half to death."

"Sorry about that, but I was driving by when I heard the engine straining. What's up?"

"I don't know what's wrong with this thing. It started just fine all day yesterday. Then this morning—" She blew a raspberry, which wasn't very ladylike but expressed her feelings perfectly.

He laughed, and she trailed after him, watching him lever open the hood and peer inside. After about five seconds, he muttered, "Don't look now, but your grandmother's eyeballing us. Think she knows enough about cars to manage some basic sabotage? Maybe hoping I'd stop and help a damsel in distress?"

Tess groaned. "Definitely. That would explain the hushed conversation she had with Chelsea last night. We already knew she and the baby were okay, so I couldn't figure out what else they'd be whispering about. When I asked Gram about it later, she pulled the innocent act on me. 'I have no idea what you're referring to, dear,'" Tess mimicked her huffy response. "She had me convinced I was overtired and my imagination was playing tricks on me. She even sent me up to my room to get a good night's sleep, like I was seven years old or something."

"That tracks with what Chelsea said to me yesterday at the mill," Heath's voice rumbled from under the rusty hood. "Apparently, she thinks we'd make a great pair."

"Of what?"

"Good one," he said, letting out another laugh.

"They're loony, both of them. Only crazy people would even think of putting us together, much less conspiring to make it happen. We're like night and day."

"No argument here." Extracting himself from the engine compartment, he took a brightly colored handkerchief from the back pocket of his jeans and wiped his hands before dropping the hood. "I think you're set now. Why don't you get in and give it a whirl?"

She did, and the truck started right up. Of course it did, she thought, glancing at the house. She couldn't see anyone, but she was confident Gram was still watching them to gauge the results of her trickery. "It's kind of sweet, really. Don't you think?"

"Sweet and sneaky," he said with a good-natured look. "Southern women can be that way, and I guess the Barretts are no exception. How 'bout you?"

"Not me. If I like you, I'll tell you straight to your face."

"And if you don't?" he asked with a grin.

"I'll tell you that, too." Pausing, she let out a sigh. "It got me in no end of trouble with my ex's family. All his sisters-in-law are the polite, proper type. When we got serious about each other, I tried everything I could think of to be more like them. I thought I did a pretty good job of fitting in, but it turned out I was wrong."

"Why would you even bother?" he demanded with a disapproving scowl.

His question sliced through her with a precision that made her hackles rise in self-defense. She told herself it had nothing to do with the fact that she'd asked herself the exact same thing at least a hundred times. "I don't see how it's any of your business."

"It's not," he admitted in a gentler tone. "But I hate to see anyone close off who they are just to try and fit in. God made us who we are for a reason, and it's up to us to figure out a way to work with what He gave us."

Tess was stunned by the little sermon. The easygoing mechanic didn't strike her as the preachy type. To be honest, she couldn't help feeling a little jealous of his certainty. Knowing there was a purpose to your life must be comforting when things got tough.

"You really believe that?" she asked. When he nodded, she frowned. "I guess I hadn't thought of it that way."

"Most folks don't, until something goes wrong. Then they start looking around and realize if they'd just had a little more faith, things would've ended up better for them."

Was that why things had gone so disastrously for her up to now? she wondered. Because she was meant to be somewhere else, or with someone else?

Or both?

Bewildered by questions she couldn't begin to answer, she shook off her brooding and forced a smile. "I'll keep that in mind. Meantime, thanks so much for your help with the truck. I'm sure the crew's already at the mill, and I'd hate to be late for work two days in a row."

"No problem." Angling his head toward the pickup, he gave her a sly look. "I got a feeling it'll start right up for you this afternoon."

"Unless Gram has an accomplice at the mill. You know she takes full credit for finally getting Paul, Jason and Scott married off, right?"

"Not Scott," Heath protested. "We've been friends forever, and he's as bullheaded as they come. When he got home from prison and started working on the old homestead, he was doing the hermit thing till he met Jenna. She turned his head all on her own."

"I'm not denying she's fabulous, but Aunt Diane told me Jenna had a little help from Gram." She waved her fingers in a mystical gesture. "Chelsea and Amy did, too, and I don't hear the boys complaining about it."

"True enough," he admitted with a grin. "Gotta admit the three of 'em did all right for a bunch of clueless hounds."

"Those shenanigans won't work with me, though. I'm onto her game, and much as I appreciate the effort, I won't be playing along."

"I don't know," he drawled, mischief twinkling in his eyes. "It might be fun."

His not-so-subtle suggestion made her laugh, and she realized she'd done that more in the past twenty-four hours than she had for months. Then again, she hadn't had much to laugh about lately. "Not a chance, country boy. You'd start off pretending, and before you knew what happened, it would all be for real. Then where would you be?"

"In love with you."

His entire demeanor had gone dead serious, and she searched those vivid blue eyes for a sign that he was yanking her chain. When she couldn't find one, her heart lurched in sheer panic. "What?"

"Gotcha." Chuckling, he winked at her. "You should see your face right now. It's the color of a bleached sheet."

"I—well—" Appalled to hear herself stammering like some brainless twit, she took a moment to get her pulse out of startled-hum-mingbird range. "Good one. You know I have to get you back now, right?"

"Wouldn't be any fun if you didn't."

"When you least expect it…"

"Yeah, yeah, yeah," he retorted, rocking his head in a derisive motion. "That's what they all say."

As he sauntered away, she found herself speechless, mouth open like a beached fish while she hunted for a decent comeback. Since she couldn't come up with anything suit-ably crushing, she shouted, "In your dreams, Weatherby!"

Without looking back, he held up his hand before climbing into what could only be de-scribed as a red mini–monster truck. Still rat-tled by their bizarre exchange, she took solace in the fact that she'd gotten the last word. Only because he'd let her, she realized while she put the sawmill truck in gear and headed in the opposite direction Heath had taken.

Still, considering the way her life had been going recently, she'd take any victory she could get.

Tess Barrett was really starting to bug him. He just didn't know why.

Pounding out the bent sheet metal on the

front fender of Olivia's sedan, Heath let his mind wander to her headstrong granddaughter for a few minutes. Their spirited exchange that morning echoed in his mind, amusing him one second and aggravating him the next. Just like she did, he realized with a scowl.

He just didn't know why.

Realizing his thoughts had begun to repeat themselves, he did his best to put them aside and focus on his work. It was tough to do when all he could think about was how the flowing pink blouse Tess was wearing today set off her eyes, not to mention the fact that she smelled like magnolias on a warm summer evening.

The iron mallet he was using slipped off the fender and nailed his thumb hard enough to jerk him back to reality. Shaking his throbbing hand, he set down the hammer and took a swig of cold water before holding the bottle against the bruise that was already forming beneath his skin.

"Man needs to pay attention when he's swinging one o' those things."

Glancing over his shoulder, Heath found his boss, Fred Morgan, watching him with a bemused look on his craggy face. He was the one who'd taken Heath under his wing as a teenager, showing him how to turn his natural-born love of all things mechanical into a job he could do anywhere. Not to mention, he'd made a spot for Heath when he returned from Alaska, no questions asked.

Chuckling at his own clumsiness, Heath got to his feet and held up his hand. "Nothing's broken, so I'll live."

"Good to hear."

"Did you need something?"

"Just making sure you're all here," Fred replied in his usual forthright way. "You seemed a little distracted when you came in this morning."

"I'm fine."

"Tess Barrett could distract a dead man out of his own grave," the older man continued with a knowing look.

"How'd you—oh, right. Your wife has binoculars."

"Technically, they're mine, but she uses 'em a lot more than I do. Just thought you oughta know the hens are watching you, so make sure you don't do anything stupid."

"Thanks for the heads-up." Heath figured saying anything more than he already had would only get him a lecture he didn't want, so he deftly changed the subject. "I made out a parts list for this monster. It's on your desk."

"I'll go call it in."

"Y'know, they've got a website where you

can enter everything yourself. You get an email confirmation and a quicker delivery date because they don't have to pay someone to answer the phone and write it all down."

Fred gave him a baffled look. "Then what happens to Edie, the nice old lady who takes down orders for them? One of the reasons I deal with them is I like talking to a person instead of punching my way through some automated menu till I finally get to the right department."

"She could spend that time doing other things."

"Like what? It's a parts warehouse. You think they're gonna teach her how to drive a forklift or something?"

Since he'd never given any thought to how their parts supplier functioned, Heath didn't have an answer for that one. "Okay, you got me there. Edie wins this round."

"Good boy. Now, get back to work before I take this break outta your lunch."

He punctuated that with a vague motion toward the jacked-up sedan then headed back to his office. While Heath did his best to go along with Fred's order, all on its own his mind circled back to the original topic of their odd discussion.

Tess.

As he resumed dissecting his unusual morning, one thing became very clear to him. In a village this size, chances were they'd be seeing a lot of each other. That meant he had to come up with a way to deflect all the unwanted attention they seemed to be attracting whenever they were together. Because if he didn't, the gossips were going to drive both of them nuts.

# *Chapter Four*

Obviously, these men were completely help-
less.

Appalled by the minimal basic skills the
sawmill's crew of carpenters seemed to pos-
sess, Tess grumbled to herself while she made
two pots of long-overdue coffee for the com-
mercial system in the lobby. The trail of donut
crumbs leading back toward the saw area told
her they'd at least managed to feed themselves,
so she got a broom from the supply closet and
swept the mess out the front door and off the
porch. Boyd and Daisy probably took care of
that on a normal day, she thought as she went
around opening windows to let in some of the
crisp fall air.

But this wasn't a normal day, and without
Chelsea here to get everything organized for
her, Tess had a lot of catching up to do. Squar-

ing her shoulders, she strode into the office and took stock. There was no point in sugarcoating it, she realized. The place was a complete wreck. Paperwork, receipts and invoices were strewn across the desk, and a light dusting of animal fur covered pretty much everything. Even though she wasn't allergic, just pawing through the layers got her sneezing, and she changed tracks. Clean first, then organize.

With the benefit of some perspective, she recognized that was what she should have done yesterday. The problem was she'd been too overwhelmed by her unfamiliar surroundings to be sensible about—well, anything. Her unhelpful deer-in-the-headlights attitude was history, and she promised herself she wasn't leaving today until everything was processed and neatly tucked in its proper place.

Chelsea's baby wasn't due for another eight weeks, and her condition was more delicate than Tess had understood until this morning. Now that she had an inkling of how the rest of the pregnancy might go, it was obvious to her that she'd have to be lighter on her feet than she was accustomed to. In the interest of beginning her new, more independent life, she'd have to learn how to cope when things went awry. It wasn't just about her anymore, and her family was counting on her to pitch in and keep the business running as smoothly as Chelsea had.

She'd never been in charge of anything before, but there was no one else to take on that responsibility. Feeling way out of her depth, she pushed her doubts away and finished tidying up the waiting area. *One task down*, she thought morosely as she reluctantly trudged into the office, *a hundred more to go*.

When Scott poked his head in the door, she snarled, "What?"

Her cousin backed up, his brown eyes narrowing in response to her mood. "Just wanted to let you know we're firing up the saws. It's gonna get pretty loud out here."

"Thanks for the warning," she replied in a slightly less cranky tone. "I'm sorry for biting your head off. It's just—"

"This place is a disaster zone, and you don't know what to tackle first," he filled in with an understanding smile. "Mostly, you're worried about Chelsea and the baby. We all are."

Tess had grown accustomed to managing life's unexpected curves on her own, and she found it comforting to know she no longer had to hide her feelings and soldier on, no matter what. "Thanks for understanding." Looking around, she muttered, "Those headphones must be somewhere."

Grinning, Scott reached around the door frame and plucked them from a hook on the wall. Exactly where Chelsea had left them, of course.

"Thanks again," she said, feeling slightly ridiculous. Fortunately, he didn't mention it, which she really appreciated.

"Sure. I'll come let you know when it's safe to take them off."

With that, he sauntered back toward the production floor, sliding the heavy door shut behind him. Built of solid oak, it blocked some of the sound but did nothing to blunt the thumping vibrations that shook the mill house while the equipment was operating at full speed. Tess focused her attention on the bookkeeping and after a while, anything that wasn't on the computer screen faded into the background. She was sorting through the online orders that had come in when she noticed the screen on her cell phone blinking with a call.

When she saw it was Paul, she ripped off her headphones and hit Answer all in one motion. "Hello?"

"Hey, Tess," he answered in an exhausted voice. "How're things going out there?"

"Oh, fine." Suddenly, she realized everything was ominously quiet, and the floorboards were no longer shuddering beneath her shoes.

With the backlog of orders lined up to be filled, that couldn't be good, but she decided not to mention it to Paul. "I assume you're calling with news."

"Yeah. We're home now, but the doctor doesn't like the looks of Chelsea's blood pressure or the baby's heartbeat. She's on bed rest for the duration, starting now."

An argument was brewing out on the shop floor, and Tess cupped her hand around the phone to keep it from reaching her worried cousin. "You sound wrung out yourself, so stay home today. We can handle this place for a day without you."

"We? It sounds like you're trying to take over my business."

"Trust me, if I was going to do that, it would be at a nice little boutique where I don't have to worry about losing my hearing," she retorted in her sauciest tone. "Your precious sawmill is safe from me."

"Good to know." She heard a muffled back and forth, then he came back on the line. "Chelsea wanted me to remind you the printer's been repaired and is waiting for you at the office supply store in town. Unless you want to write everything down by hand for the crew, you'll need it."

Tess swallowed a groan of frustration.

Apparently, this was going to be one of those days. "Right. Now go get some rest and I'll see you tomorrow."

"Actually, if you can make do without me, I'd like to take Thursday and Friday off, too. Chelsea can't go up and down the stairs for the next few weeks, so I have to hurry up and finish the extra bathroom I've been working on to get everything she needs on the ground floor."

"Not a problem," Tess assured him, hoping she came across as more confident than she actually felt. "Chelsea and the baby come first. Take all the time you need."

"We're not going anywhere, so call if you get stuck on something."

"Will do."

After she hung up, she summoned every ounce of her patience and went to see what the fuss in the back room was about. The sliding door was even heavier than it looked, and it took a determined push for her to get it open. Once she did, she wished she hadn't.

It looked like several pieces of machinery had exploded at once, spewing oil over everything from the equipment to the hewn lumber that had been stacked according to size in the center of the room. Scott and Jason hadn't escaped the deluge, and they were standing by the long saw run, arms folded stubbornly while they glowered at each other and debated what to do. As their argument escalated into an all-out shouting match, she shook her head in disgust.

Boys. No matter how old they got, they could still be the dumbest creatures on the planet. Since they didn't seem to understand that yelling wouldn't solve anything, she strode in to impose some kind of order. She waited a few seconds for them to notice her then realized they'd probably go on like this until one of them either conceded or ran out of air. Being Barretts, neither of those was likely to happen anytime soon.

Filling her lungs, she yelled, "Hey!" That didn't make an impression, so she tried again. "Shut up!"

Nothing. Exasperated beyond belief, she recalled the advice her grandmother had given her earlier and went for broke. "If you two morons don't cut it out, I'm calling Gram."

That one got through, and her ears rang in the sudden quiet. Shaking her head to clear them, she went on. "Will you please tell me what has you guys at each other's throats?"

They started in together, and she held up her hands. "One at a time. Start with explaining to me why the saws aren't running."

They glared at each other, but fortunately, Jason backed down. "You're older. You go first."

"As you can see," Scott began with a dismissive motion toward the archaic equipment, "everything went haywire. Paul's the only one who knows how to fix this relic, so I think we should call him."

"And I don't," Jason chimed in, his jaw set with determination. "He needs to be with Chelsea right now, not worrying about this place."

"You're both right." While she relayed her brief conversation with their big brother, she watched as their obstinate expressions gave way to worry. "Isn't there someone else on the crew who can help with this?"

"Hank and Joe are gone all week for their annual fishing trip," Scott replied. "We've got part-timers starting up next week, but we can't run any more raw material without the saws. If we can't figure out how to get them running, we'll have to close down till one of those three comes back."

Tess was hardly a manufacturing expert, but she understood that losing even a day or two of production this time of year would be a major setback for any business that was so reliant on the holidays for their annual revenue. Judging by the spreadsheets she'd been working on, profit margins at the sawmill were razor-thin as it was. If they lost any ground at all, the company her family had fought so hard to resurrect might very well end up back in bankruptcy.

It wasn't only the Barretts who relied on sales of the custom furniture for their income, she knew. While the small staff of carpenters and assemblers worked only part-time, for many of them the extra money they earned made the difference between living comfortably and barely scraping by.

"You're the college girl," Jason teased her with a grin. "Any ideas?"

"No, I—" Inspiration struck, and she snapped her fingers. "What about Heath?"

"Mechanical genius," Scott agreed, "but he's got a job, remember?"

"Maybe I can talk Fred into giving him the afternoon off. You know, as a favor to us."

"I'm married to his niece," Jason pointed out. "So I'm practically family. I can go into town right now and ask him."

His older brother vetoed that idea with a firm shake of his head. "You'll stop by to have lunch with Amy, and I won't see you the rest of the day. I can't run this place by myself, y'know."

Considering how they'd been going at it just a few minutes ago, Tess expected that to start another argument. To her relief, Jason conceded with a sheepish grin.

"Okay, you got me there," he admitted. "Guess that means it's up to you, Tess. Meantime, we'll go outside and get some fresh lumber ready to go."

In the time she'd spent getting to know the Southern branch of her family, she'd learned that was the Barrett spirit. They took their best run at Plan A, but if that didn't work, they regrouped and tried something else. While she headed back to the office, it occurred to her that she must have inherited some of that natural resilience, too. If she could find a way to tap into it, maybe it would help her reboot her life. Solving this particular problem might not be a huge deal to some people, but for her it was definitely a step in the right direction.

It occurred to her that none of them had questioned whether or not Heath would agree to lend a hand with the cranky old machinery. Where she was from, that kind of assumption could get you in all kinds of trouble, but it seemed that here people pitched in when and where they could. She only hoped that once he diagnosed the problem, Heath didn't discover he'd taken on more than he bargained for.

She was about to dial the number for Morgan's Garage when another thought materialized. This wasn't Los Angeles, it was Barrett's Mill. Around here, folks probably didn't ask for this kind of special consideration via email or over the phone. Basically, Fred would be giving up an afternoon of Heath's valuable time, reassigning those jobs so his employee could go help someone else. If she wanted to do it right, she'd go in person.

She had to pick up the printer anyway, she reasoned as she got her purse and went out to the truck. While she was in town, she'd get some lunch for all of them. With the way things had gone today, it would be nice to eat something more than sandwiches out of paper bags.

Driving toward the main road, she glanced at the mill in the rearview mirror and allowed herself a little smile. She'd been here only a couple of days, but already she was actively involved in the family business. After being consumed by the fateful twists and turns she'd been trying to navigate, she'd finally taken off the blinders to find that her life held much more potential than she'd realized.

And it felt wonderful.

Even though it was late morning now, she had no trouble finding a parking spot near Mill Office Supply. Just another difference between the crowded streets she was used to and this charming village. No circling the block waiting for someone to pull out of a space barely long enough to accommodate a compact car. When she got back to LA, she'd have to remember to brush up on her parallel parking. She didn't doubt that after a two-month break, she'd be sorely out of practice.

Inside the shop, she found the clerk perched on top of a ladder, arranging binders and composition books on one of the higher shelves. "Good morning."

"Hang on just a sec," she replied, taking the last few notebooks out of the box before dropping it to the floor. Brushing off her hands, she descended the steps and gave Tess a bright, helpful smile. "What can I do for you?"

"I'm Tess Barrett, and I—"

"Oh, I know who you are." Laughing, the friendly young woman offered a hand. "Paige Donaldson. I've heard all about you from my grandma Lila. She and your gram are like this." She twined her index and middle fingers together like a pretzel. "How are you liking our little town so far?"

"It's beautiful," Tess replied with sincere enthusiasm. In the short time she'd been here, her father's hometown had really grown on her. "And the people are so friendly."

"That's us," Paige agreed with a bright

smile. "Beautiful and friendly. I'd imagine you're here to pick up that printer Chelsea dropped off last week. How's she doing, by the way?"

Unsure of how much to say, Tess opted to keep her response vague. "The doctor's keeping a close eye on her and the baby."

"Well, next time you see her, tell her we're all keeping her, Paul and the baby in our prayers. And give her a hug from me."

Again with the praying. She'd encountered more religious people in the past few days than she had her entire life, and she couldn't help wondering if maybe they had the right idea, after all. Tabling the possibility for another time, Tess thanked her and wandered through the aisles while she waited. She picked up a few odds and ends for the office and met Paige back at the counter.

"These holiday brochures were ready early, so that saves you a trip," the clerk announced cheerfully, patting a box that sported a label from a print shop located in nearby Cambridge.

"Great. I'll take a look at them when I get back."

They settled the bill and Paige helped her lug everything outside. When she got a look at Tess's wheels, she laughed. "This truck's like a hot potato in your family, isn't it?"

"I guess it is," she agreed. "As long as Heath can keep it running, anyway."

"He's notorious around here. There's not a girl within fifty miles who could walk past that man and not take a second look."

Did he look back? Tess wondered before she could stop herself. They barely knew each other, so it was absolutely none of her business who he admired or ignored. She wasn't normally the jealous type, so her reaction made no sense whatsoever. Then again, so little in her life made sense these days, she'd kind of gotten used to it.

"Is that right?" she asked to be polite.

"Oh, don't get me wrong," Paige added hastily. "He's a great guy, but we're more like cousins than anything. But if he ever took it into his head to change that, he wouldn't have to ask me twice."

She punctuated her confession with a wink, and Tess wasn't sure how to respond. Finally, she settled for a nod and a quick good-bye before heading for the other side of town.

Before she knew it, she was making the turn into Morgan's Garage. She didn't find its owner in his office, but in one of the large bays, wrestling lug nuts from the tire of a delivery truck whose bright color made it look like a huge lemon on wheels. When Fred caught sight of her, he rose to his feet, wiping his hands on a rag he took from his back pocket. The motion reminded her of Heath, and Tess firmly brought her mind back to her very important mission.

"Mornin', Tess." Well-lined from what she assumed was a lifetime spent outside, Fred's weathered cheeks crinkled with a smile. "It's not often we get treated to such a pretty view in here. How're things with you?"

Since coming to Barrett's Mill, she'd been asked that more times than she could count. She was gradually getting accustomed to it, and she had a smile ready for him. "Aside from the time difference, I'm doing well. How about you?"

"Can't complain, and if I did nobody'd listen, anyway." With a good-natured chortle, he continued. "Olivia's car needs more work than we thought at first. Parts are on their way, but it'll be out of commission another day or two."

"I'll tell her later, but that's not why I'm here."

While she outlined her reason for coming, he gave her a frown that said he could easily relate to what they were going through. "Of course you can have him. That mill's real important to folks around here, so we need to get it up and running. I'll go fetch him for you on one condition."

In her experience, conditions weren't good for the one asking the favor. But the boys were in a jam, and beyond dragging Paul away from his ailing wife, she didn't see any other options. Knowing how devoted he was to the family business, she suspected he'd agree to just about anything to get the benefit of Heath's expertise, so she braced herself for Fred's terms. "Okay."

"If this turns out to be over Heath's head, give me a call."

"I'm sorry?" she said, totally confused.

"My granddaddy—God rest him—worked his whole career as a sawyer at that mill, raised six kids and had a good life because of the Barretts. Come to think of it, if you need me, I'll be happy to come out and lend a hand myself."

The sweet, generous offer just about floored her, and it took all she had not to gape at him. She'd never been around people who stepped up when things got tough for their neighbors, simply because it was the right thing to do. Even before his niece married Jason, Fred had felt a kinship with her family and was willing to put aside his own obligations to help them out. Beyond tradition, it was something she'd seen so rarely, she almost didn't recognize it.

Honor.

Humbled and gratified all at once, she beamed at him. Suspecting he wouldn't take kindly to any feminine gushing, she kept it simple. "Thank you, Fred. I'll let Scott and Jason know."

With a brisk nod, he headed out the large front door and around the side of the building. While she waited, she went out to the mill truck and took one of the freshly printed brochures from the box Paige had given her. Leafing through the matte pages, she admired the way it was laid out with more pictures than text. It gave the impression that you were strolling through the display area of the mill yourself, rather than just reading about it.

Boyd and Daisy were featured in several of the pictures, and while the folksy approach was nice enough, she wondered if there was a better way to showcase the company's offerings. The current material might speak to buyers who lived in the country, but many city dwellers might consider it hokey and not look past the presentation to appreciate the superior quality of the handcrafted furniture.

"Nice, huh?"

Heath's voice descended on her from nowhere, and she jerked back in surprise, turning her ankle in the process. Her high heel buckled underneath her, and she instinctively started windmilling, desperately grasping for something to keep her from falling.

Just when she was convinced she was doomed to hit the pavement, two strong arms reached out and rescued her. Heath guided her to her feet as if she didn't weigh a thing, circling his arms around her to keep her steady.

"Are you okay?" he asked.

It was the second time she'd heard that from him in as many days, and it was getting old. With her heart trying to slam its way out of her chest, she took a couple of deep breaths to regain her usual composure. Just when she thought she had a grip on her nerves, she looked up.

A pair of warm blue eyes gazed back at her, filled with an emotion she couldn't begin to define. Not concern, but not humor, either, it was a look she hadn't yet seen from him. Or from anyone else, for that matter.

*Get a grip, Tess*, she scolded herself impatiently. *Say something.* "Yes."

Her answer was more clipped than she'd intended it to be, and she regretted the dimming effect it had on him. Releasing her, he took a step back. A big one.

"Fred said you wanted to talk to me."

For a few moments she couldn't recall why.

Then it came to her, and she felt her cheeks warming with embarrassment. She was acting like a teenager with a crush on the school's star running back, she realized, disgusted by her own foolishness.

While she explained why she'd crashed his day, he listened carefully, nodding and frowning in all the right places. Avery had never paid such close attention to anything she'd said, and she had to admit that despite the serious nature of her errand, she liked being treated with so much respect.

When she was finished, he gave her a bewildered look. "I can come out and take a look, but I don't know much about nineteenth-century gadgets. It could take me a while."

"While you get your tools together, I'll head over to The Whistlestop to pick up lunch for the boys. I can add an order for you, if you want."

"I've got my own lunch." Mischief glinted in his eyes, and he stepped closer. "But I don't wanna eat in the middle of all that sawdust."

The playful twinkle she'd noticed warmed with something entirely different, and she couldn't drag her eyes away. Not that she tried very hard. Thankfully, logic broke into her daze and kick-started her brain. "The office is still a mess, but you're welcome to eat in there."

She heard the stiffness in her tone and barely managed not to cringe. That was the cool, professional voice she'd cultivated for difficult customers, and it was sorely out of place here. Since she couldn't take it back, the only thing she could do was hope that Heath wouldn't notice.

Unfortunately, his scowl made it clear that he noticed everything. "Actually, I was thinking we could eat lunch together. After our conversation this morning, I thought you were warming up to me. Am I wrong?"

Was that the impression she'd been giving him? Tess wondered. Taking a moment to think it over, she realized she was standing as far from him as she could, arms crossed in a defensive gesture she hadn't been aware of until now. What on earth was wrong with her? He was an old family friend who'd generously agreed to leave his paying job and drive out into the woods to help them. She should be embracing him, not giving him a hard time.

Then again, hugging him wasn't the brightest notion she'd ever had, and she reminded herself of her vow to keep him at a safe, friendly distance. Summoning her brightest smile, she said, "Not a bit. I'm just a little out of sorts is all. It's been an eventful morning."

"You don't have to pretend everything's okay, Tess," he murmured, sympathy flooding his eyes. "Take my word on this one—it doesn't work for very long."

"I'm making do."

Studying her for several long, uncomfortable moments, he slowly shook his head. "You wanna lie to me, fine. Just make sure you're being honest with yourself."

The drive out to the mill was uncomfortable, to say the least.

Tess didn't glance at him even once, and the firm set of her delicate jaw told him in no uncertain terms that his comment about honesty had hit a very sore spot. It underscored his belief that she was hiding something from her family, but he figured now wasn't the time to try to shoehorn any closely held secrets from her.

Now was the time to apologize. He'd learned long ago that when it came to women, it didn't matter who was wrong and who was right. What counted was who made the amends. So he swallowed his pride and said, "Tess, I'm sorry. I didn't mean to upset you."

"You didn't."

The airy tone was obviously meant as a verbal brush-off, but her stony expression told him otherwise.

Least said, soonest mended. His grandmother's wise advice echoed in his memory, and he decided to follow it. If Tess wanted to take up the subject with him again in the future, she knew where to find him.

When they reached the mill, she couldn't get away from him fast enough. Bolting from the truck, she went up the steps and into the lobby, shoulders stiff and her cute little nose in the air. He suspected that if the screen door would've cooperated, she would've slammed it for good measure.

Leaving Tess and her puzzling attitude behind, he strode toward the lumberyard and was greeted by a rousing cheer. He acknowledged their enthusiastic welcome then held up his hands in a calming gesture. "Okay, boys, what've you done now?"

"We've got no clue," Scott admitted in the same direct way he'd used since they'd squared off on the playground in kindergarten, each determined to be the first one to go down the new slide. When they weren't looking, Jimmy Griggs had scampered up the ladder and skunked them both. Angry at being outdone by their quick-thinking classmate, Heath and Scott had been friends ever since.

"Everything's covered in oil," Jason chimed in. "Does that help?"

"Maybe," Heath allowed, going onto the bridge to inspect the mechanism that ran the waterwheel. His first thought was that some debris that had floated downstream might be caught in the paddles or the dam opening, but they were clear. Since everything looked okay outside, the three of them went up the side steps that led into the saw room. When he got a glimpse of the mess, he groaned.

"Yeah, that's what we said, too," Scott told him with a grim look. "It's bad, isn't it?"

"It's not good, that's for sure." He wouldn't be needing any tools until he could figure out what to fix, so he set his box down on the side porch to keep it clean. "Anything else I should know?"

"Isn't this enough?" Jason added a wry grin. "If you're looking for more of a challenge, we could go break something else for you."

"No, I'm good. Just get outta my way and let me work."

Laughing, they turned and went back to the rough-cut station. The massive saw hanging in its stocks looked as if it could take down a whole forest if you left it running, and Heath marveled at how deftly they operated the lethal-looking machine. He was pretty coordinated himself, but you couldn't have paid him enough to run that thing.

Inside, he started with a pile of rags and enough degreaser to choke an elephant. When the equipment was as clean as he could get it, he stood in front of the parallel saw runs and studied the works carefully. Long leather belts were looped over a complex system of pulleys and rollers, leading down to the floor where they were engaged by a wooden lever that went through an opening in the floor to the waterwheel.

Based on very grim experience, he knew this setup was a tragedy waiting to happen. Grabbing an empty cardboard box, he broke it down to form a shield that he placed over the handle and nailed to the wall behind it. In the storeroom he found some huge markers used for labeling boxes. He snagged one and finished his safety warning in large, bold letters.

DO NOT USE WHEEL—HEATH

He was adding the date when he heard soft footsteps coming up behind him. Turning, he saw Tess, carrying an armful of leather-bound books and wearing what appeared to be a pair of well-loved leather moccasins. Hoping to break their icy impasse, he chuckled. "I'm thinking that's not the look your Beverly Hills designer was after."

To his great relief, she laughed and held out her foot to admire the slipper. "I found them under the old woodstove in the office. I thought they worked."

"What happened to your fancy Italian shoes?"

"One of the heels is broken. And they're from Paris, thank you very much." The sassy tone went perfectly with the spark in her eyes, and he was glad to see she seemed to have recovered from their earlier skirmish. He just wished he could say the same about himself.

If he brought it up, she'd have the perfect opening to blast him again. But he'd obviously hurt her, and he knew he wouldn't be able to sleep if he didn't at least try to make things right with her.

Moving toward her, he took a deep breath and braced himself for a good old-fashioned dressing down. "Tess, I was outta line earlier. I'm real sorry."

As if he'd flipped some unseen switch, her eyes narrowed with that infamous Barrett temper, and she met him in the middle of the floor. Most folks were intimidated by his size, whether or not they'd come out and admit it. But not this woman, he noticed with honest admiration. They were steel toe to moccasin, staring at each other, and she hadn't even flinched.

"No one talks to me that way," she informed him in a calm voice that seemed very much at odds with her steely glare. Then, in the space it took him to blink, that harsh look mellowed into something else entirely, and she gave him a grateful smile. "Thank you."

"Excuse me?" Having prepared himself for a scolding, he was convinced he hadn't heard that right.

"I needed to hear it, but the family walks on eggshells around me, afraid to say the wrong thing. I'm sure they'll appreciate you taking the hit for them," she added with a wry grin.

"So you're not mad?"

"Oh, I'm mad," she corrected him sweetly. "But you were right, and I'm grown up enough to admit that."

Considering how badly their touchy conversation might have gone, this result suited him much better. Heath decided it was best to leave things as they were and move forward from here. Tapping one of the ledgers she held, he asked, "What're these?"

"Maintenance logs for everything from the old adding machines to these monsters in here. They go back to when the mill was first built, and Chelsea keeps them in the lobby display for folks to leaf through. I thought you might find something helpful in them."

"Great idea," he approved, shaking his head with a grin. "Why didn't I think of that?"

She made a show of looking at the beamed ceiling, searching for the answer. When her eyes landed back on him, they glittered in fun. "Because men have a genetic aversion to reading instructions?"

"Got me there, magpie."

As she handed over the manuals, she tilted her head with a puzzled expression. "What did you call me?"

"Magpie. You can find them in Canada, which is where I know them from. They're pretty birds that always seem to have a lot to say." It occurred to him that the assessment might not appeal to her, and he said, "You remind me of one, but if you don't like it, I'll quit."

"No, I like it. It's just that I've never had a nickname before."

"Why not?"

"I guess no one ever cared enough to give me one."

Her wistful look made him want to take her in his arms and remind her that whatever bad things had happened to her were safely locked in the past. He managed not to do it, but it was a near thing. As he watched her stroll back through the door, a single disturbing thought was blaring like an alarm siren in his mind.

Man, was he in trouble.

# Chapter Five

It was long past dark by the time Tess caught up with everything she needed to do. Chelsea hadn't been kidding about the amount of work that had been piling up, she thought as she stood and stretched out her sore back. It didn't help that she was unfamiliar with the software, and Paul's pathological disorganization was a constant roadblock. Actually, she admitted with a sigh, when she first got started she had no clue what she was doing. But now she was an expert in the quirky ways of Barrett's Mill Furniture.

Maybe she could stay on a while longer, give Chelsea more time at home with the new baby. Tess had always been a worker bee, far from the decision-making levels of the companies she'd worked for. Despite her ongoing fear of messing up something important, she was surprised to find she relished the challenge of setting her own pace and learning as she went along. While she wouldn't enjoy the same security—or salary—as she would at a more established business, here at the mill she'd have something much more important.

Independence.

The alternate life she'd stumbled into was full of opportunities to prove herself, and she couldn't deny it held a solid appeal for her. Each time she tackled something foreign to her and succeeded, her confidence level rose a bit more. If she kept improving the way she hoped to, she might even discover a path to the self-sufficient existence she craved. With no attachments to anyone in particular, she could pretty much go anywhere she wanted. Wouldn't it be something if she found what she'd been looking for in the hometown her father had abandoned so long ago?

While she was straightening up the office, she heard the unmistakable creaks and squeals of the vintage machinery grinding into action. Standing with a sheaf of invoices in her hands, she held her breath, but the sounds died down as quickly as they'd sprung up. After some inventive insults and a couple more tries, the familiar thrumming noise of the drive belts settled into the rhythmic sound that told anyone with half a brain that Barrett's Sawmill was up and running again.

A rousing cheer went up in the rear of the old mill house, and she went back to find three very grimy men hooting and jumping around like six-year-olds who'd just won a baseball game. She smiled as they traded greasy high fives but hesitated when Heath offered her one.

He cocked his head in a chiding gesture, and she laughed. "Oh, why not?" She noticed he was much gentler with her than he'd been with her cousins, which she appreciated. Looking around, she marveled at the belts slinging through their paces as if nothing had ever stopped them. "This is fabulous, guys. What did you end up doing?"

"A little of everything," Heath answered in a voice that was equal parts tired and proud. "Those maintenance manuals you found are worth their weight in gold, so make sure you put 'em somewhere safe."

"Will do. I hate to bring this up," she added with a hesitant look around, "but this place is a mess. Should I call the crew and tell them to stay home again tomorrow?"

"Not a chance," Jason replied with a determined shake of his head. "We can't lose another day, so we'll get it cleaned up somehow."

"Would you like some help?"

The three of them looked toward the door, where Amy and Jenna—the newest Mrs. Barretts—stood holding all manner of cleaning supplies. Jason's wife, Amy, set down the mops and paper towels she was holding, while Jenna plunked down two enormous buckets filled with cleaning solvent from the studio she shared with Scott.

Wow, Tess thought with genuine admiration for her friend. The slender artist was a lot stronger than she looked.

"But first," Amy announced in the authoritative voice of someone who spent her days teaching kids to dance, "we eat."

"That sounds great," Jason told her with a quick hug, "but we emptied the fridge around four."

"Oo, shocker," Jenna teased with a bright laugh. "Good thing we already guessed that."

Linking arms with Scott, she led them through the lobby and out to one of the picnic tables where tourists ate when they visited the old mill. Spread on top was a checkered tablecloth that held everything from pork to ham to two apple pies steaming in the cool evening air. All thickly sliced, of course.

"Olivia's over at Paul and Chelsea's with your mom, whipping everything into shape," Jenna explained. "But she didn't forget about all of you slaving away out here. As soon as she heard what was going on, she started cooking."

"Man, she's the best." Heath sighed as he sank down onto a bench beside the other two who were busy piling food onto their plates. "I'll have to come up with a way to thank her. Think she'd like a sunroof on her car?"

They all laughed at that then spent the next few minutes passing dishes and filling glasses. Suddenly, Tess had a sobering thought. "Paul doesn't know about these awful equipment problems, does he?"

"Absolutely not," Amy replied. "None of the family will tell him, and Aunt Helen's making sure everyone in town keeps quiet. As far as Paul and Chelsea know, this place is running like a top and they don't have a thing to worry about."

"Except the baby," Jason said quietly.

That stopped the lighthearted conversation in its tracks, and he silently held out one hand to his wife and the other to his brother sitting beside him. The others followed his lead, and despite her earlier misgivings, Tess went along without a second thought. Bowing her head, she silently introduced herself to God and sent up a heartfelt prayer for the littlest Barrett. While no one spoke, the love circling around that table set in the woods was like a living thing, wrapping her in the kind of warmth she'd never experienced before.

This was how it felt to belong somewhere, she realized. To be surrounded by solid, down-to-earth folks who valued each other above everything else in the world. Not money, not prestige, but people. Lavish parties and decadent weekends away with Avery had been fun at first, but after a while they'd gotten to be just one more stuffy obligation she had to meet. Struggling to fit into his lofty world, she'd gradually forgotten what it was like to enjoy a spontaneous girls' night out with her friends.

As the others raised their heads and began eating, Tess's heart swelled with gratitude to them for making her feel so welcome. She was as new to them as they were to her, but they'd gone out of their way to make her feel like one of the crew.

"So, Tess," Jenna said while spooning potato salad onto her plate. "How's the scarecrow display coming?"

"What scarecrow display?"

"Oh, man," Heath groaned. "Chelsea forgot to tell you about it?"

"Things have been insane since I got here,"

Tess reminded him curtly. "It's not like I sit in the office buffing my nails all day, you know."

She added a cool stare for good measure, but it didn't make much impact on the easy-going mechanic. Totally unfazed, he grinned back. "The Harvest Festival is the first weekend in November. All the businesses in town put up scarecrows in the square, and folks vote on which one's the prettiest, the scariest, stuff like that."

Waiting for the punch line, she simply blinked at him. When he didn't laugh, she sighed in resignation. "You're serious, aren't you?"

"Yeah. But with everything your family has going on, I'm sure the committee will understand if the mill skips it this year."

*Her family.* The people she'd met for the first time only a month ago, who'd taken her in like a long-lost child and made a place for someone who'd never felt at home anywhere. If her father hadn't been so determined to leave his humble roots behind, she thought bitterly, she would have become acquainted with her raucous Southern cousins long ago, maybe even spent part of her summer vacations here. Riding around in pickup trucks, hanging out at the watering hole they all spoke of so fondly, enjoying impromptu picnics like this.

Through no fault of her own, she'd missed out on all of that. Hokey as the decorating contest sounded to her, if she backed out of it she knew she'd be letting her relatives down. She wasn't about to compound Dad's selfish mistakes with a completely avoidable one of her own. "Well, I still have a few weeks left to get something together. I'm sure I can figure out a way to make it work."

"We'll all help," Heath assured her with his you-can-count-on-me grin. In the short time she'd known him, it had become a familiar sight. She wasn't sure if he was like that with everyone, or if he sensed that she needed an extra dose of encouragement. Whatever the reason, she was glad he'd stepped up yet again. And this time she didn't even need to ask.

"Whattya mean *we*?" Scott growled, although a glimmer in his dark eyes gave him away. "I got more than enough to do as it is."

Taking up the challenge, Tess fired back. "Fine. Heath and I will do it ourselves. Too many hands just make a mess of things, anyway."

"Meaning she wants to be in charge." Jason chuckled, angling a look at Heath. "Think you can handle taking orders from surfer girl over there?"

Gazing across the table at her, Heath seemed

to consider the question carefully before nodding. "I think I can manage."

As the discussion swung around to other less controversial topics, Tess puzzled over Heath's reaction to her cousin's teasing. Even though he was clearly the kind of man who didn't shirk from taking the reins, he hadn't bothered to debate who'd be heading up the scarecrow project. He seemed comfortable with her taking the lead role, which was a new experience for her. More than once, her father had referred to her as his little orchid, lovely to look at but best suited to a sheltered greenhouse.

Until now, she amended firmly. If she'd learned anything in the past few months, it was that relying on others to care for her was risky, at best. At worst, it led to the kind of disaster that had driven her across the country, hoping to stumble across the mysterious something that she needed to fill the hole in her life.

She hadn't even realized she was missing anything until Scott and Jenna's wedding. But now that she recognized the gap for what it was, it wasn't the kind of thing she could ignore. Once she identified the root cause of her problem, she was confident she'd know how to solve it.

One thing she knew for sure: she was done pretending everything was fine when it wasn't.

The fact that Heath had advised her to do just that had nothing to do with her newfound determination, she assured herself. Nothing at all.

Something was up with Tess.

Even while they were all chatting and laughing, he slid a glance at her now and then, wondering if he should be worried. She was smiling in all the right places, but the expression had an absent look to it, as if her thoughts kept wandering to something else altogether. That quick mind of hers impressed him beyond words, and tonight he felt like he was at a serious disadvantage.

That was why he generally avoided getting involved with smart women, he reminded himself wryly. They were always a step or two ahead of him, if not more, and they always got tired of waiting for him to catch up. Just one more reason to keep Tess at arm's length.

The problem was, that didn't keep him from noticing how her eyes sparkled in the porch light, or how she put an extra spoonful of whipped cream on the slice of apple pie she handed over to him. When she added one of those dazzling smiles, he felt his resolve wavering and did his best to rein in his errant thoughts. He almost managed it, but not quite.

"Thanks," he said as he forked up a mouthful of Olivia's award-winning dessert.

"You're welcome. After all you've done for us today, you should have this whole pie to yourself."

Jason and Scott made choking noises, even as their wives kicked them under the table. Ignoring them, Heath grinned at Tess. It wasn't his imagination this time, he was certain. She was starting to like him. And even though he knew better, he couldn't deny he was starting to like her, too. "Maybe you can make me another one."

"Me?" Laughing as if he'd just told her the best joke she ever heard, she shook her head. "Not unless you want to land in the hospital with food poisoning. I'm the kind of girl who makes reservations, not dinner."

"Technically, this is dessert," he pointed out, bobbing his loaded fork in emphasis.

"I don't do that, either. Trust me, it's safer for everyone that way."

Heath was aware that the two married couples were subtly retreating, leaving the two of them alone beneath one of the oak trees that had been on the site since the original mill was built just after the Civil War. Its bare branches spread out overhead, showing off the stars that were coming to life in the dark sky.

Resting his arms on the table, he focused back on her. It wasn't tough, since she was the nicest view he'd had all day. "I guess this is a little more rustic than what you're used to."

"True, but it's also more fun."

"Seriously? You'd rather be here than at a sushi bar or some high-end bistro?"

Fixing those incredible eyes on him, she said, "I'd rather be here than anywhere else I can think of. Can you keep a secret?"

"Scout's honor," he replied, solemnly holding up his hand.

"Even before I lost my job," she confided while swirling the ice in her cup, "I wasn't all that happy."

The urge to say *I knew it* was almost irresistible, but he suspected it would go over better if he offered a sympathetic ear instead of gloating about being right. "Why?"

"Lots of reasons," she admitted with a delicate shrug. She refused to meet his eyes, which told him another of his hunches was correct. She was hiding something, and not only from him. Letting out a heavy sigh, she lifted her gaze to his and allowed him to see the raw emotion swirling through her eyes. "After Avery and I were together about a year, we found out I was pregnant."

Heath was glad he was sitting down, or he'd

have dropped from shock. When he recovered enough to think clearly, he understood what she was trying not to say. "You lost the baby."

Tears flooded her eyes, and she nodded before looking down at the table. Without thinking, he reached out and covered her hand with his, giving a light, reassuring squeeze.

"I guess he thought it was his out." Sniffling, she went on. "When I was going to be the mother of his child, he was only too happy to marry me. When that changed, so did he."

"I doubt that," Heath spat, struggling to keep a grip on his temper. "I've met plenty of guys like him, and rich or poor they're all the same. When the going's easy, they're fine. Give 'em a problem or two, and they're gone. He didn't deserve you, and you're better off without him."

To his surprise, she settled her palm over their stacked hands and gave him the bravest smile he'd ever seen. "How is it," she asked in a watery voice, "that someone I just met knows exactly what to say to make me feel better?"

"Practice," he admitted, seeking to lighten the mood with a rueful grin. "I'll do anything to keep a lady from crying."

That got him a hiccupping laugh, and then she got serious again. "So now you see why I'm so worried about Chelsea. She's much further along than I was, feeling the baby kick and move, setting up a nursery and everything. I can't imagine how tragic it would be for them to lose their child now."

"You were praying with us earlier," he pointed out gently. "The rest of your family's doing the same, along with everyone else in town. Don't you think that'll help?"

"I hope so."

It was obvious she didn't share his faith in the Almighty, and he seized the opportunity to nudge her toward something that could only make her life better. "Maybe you'd feel more confident about it if you talked to God more often."

"You mean, like go to church?" When he nodded, she frowned. "I don't know. Gram invited me, but it's already been a long week and I'm really looking forward to sleeping in Sunday morning."

Hearing more than reluctance in her excuse, Heath instantly backed off. In his experience, people didn't respond well to being pressured into doing something that didn't come naturally to them. This was a very personal decision for Tess, and he'd never dream of trying to coerce her into attending a service.

"No problem," he said. "If you change your mind, we'll be at the Crossroads Church at the end of Main Street."

"I'll keep that in mind."

Her extremely polite tone warned him it was time to drop the subject. "So, any ideas for the harvest display?"

"Does it really have to be scarecrows?" When he nodded, she grimaced but went on. "The only one I've ever seen up close was in *The Wizard of Oz.*"

Her little grin told him she was exaggerating, and he chuckled. "Not many scarecrows on Rodeo Drive, huh?"

"Not unless you count our customers. Some of those women had been nipped and tucked to within an inch of their lives. They were just so…"

"Phony?" he suggested when she seemed at a loss for words.

"Yeah, that's it." Sighing, she added, "I don't mean to sound melodramatic about it, but sometimes I wondered if anyone I knew was who they claimed to be."

"That'd be a problem for someone like you. You're too down-to-earth for all that nonsense."

"I don't know about that."

Despite the protest, there was a hopeful glimmer in her dark eyes, as if she really wanted to believe him. Since right now he knew her extended family better than she did, he searched for a way to prove it to her. Inspiration struck, and he said, "I think you've got a lot more country in you than you realize."

"I'm not following you."

"Look around this place," he continued, leaning his arms on the table. "What word comes to mind?"

She glanced into the woods then circled back to the mill house and its steadily thrumming waterwheel. The nearly black sky was sprinkled with stars, and as she looked up, a gentle smile played over her refined features. "Peaceful."

In that single word, he heard a lot more than she'd probably meant to tell him. He'd met a lot of people during his travels, and their stories had always intrigued him. It made him sad to know that the beautiful woman sitting across from him was carrying such a heavy burden all by herself. More than once, she'd referred to her busy life in LA, and not in a good way. It made him wonder if she might consider chucking that glittering existence in favor of something calmer.

Like Barrett's Mill.

The thought jumped into his mind on its own, startling him with the possibility of Tess being around much longer than he'd anticipated. He still had no intention of getting serious with anyone just now, but he knew that if Tess stayed in town, sticking with that plan could prove to be extremely difficult for him. Who was he kidding? Smart and sassy, she fascinated him on a regular basis. Steering clear of her would be downright impossible.

"So," she began as she scooped up the last bit of pie filling. "Now that we're sharing, I'm curious what brought you back here after all these years."

"There's really not that much to tell."

Meeting his eyes over the camping lantern in the center of the table, she pinned him with a look that clearly said she knew otherwise. "I noticed you rubbing your shoulder earlier. Were you hurt up in Alaska?"

That she'd come so close to the truth rattled him pretty hard, but he managed to nod. "Yeah."

"What happened?"

"I was working on one of those big oil rigs, and there was an explosion." Only his parents knew what had brought him back to Virginia, but once he kicked the door open, the whole story came pouring out. "Four guys died in the fire, and a dozen others were badly injured. I was on my way off the platform when it happened, so I got blown clear of the worst of it. The whole thing shook me up pretty bad."

"I can only imagine," she murmured in a tone laced with sympathy. "What a horrible thing to go through."

"I was in shock, I guess, 'cause I don't remember the EMTs taking me to the hospital. I spent a few days there, and when the doctor cleared me to leave, I got in a taxi and went straight to the airport. Didn't even know where I was going." Months later, the stench of smoke and burning oil was still fresh in his memory, and he took a deep breath, reminding himself the chaos was all in his head. "At the ticket counter, the clerk asked me where I wanted to go, and at first I had no clue. She was an older woman, and I half expected her to call security to come get this nutcase bandaged up like a mummy, but she didn't. Instead, she smiled at me and asked if I wanted to go home. That clicked for me, and she got me the last seat on a flight that ended up in Roanoke."

He hadn't told anyone—not even his parents—that part of the story. Reliving it choked him up more than he cared to admit. Glancing over at Tess, he noticed her own chin quivering before she firmed it into a smile. "I'm glad she did. After a tragedy like that, you need to be where you feel safe and can be around people who care about you."

In all honesty, he sometimes felt like he'd

run away from home at eighteen, and when the world kicked him a little too hard, he'd come crawling back. Fearing that might make her feel worse about her own circumstances, he decided it was best to keep that detail to himself.

While they'd been talking, a spirited argument had broken out inside the mill house, and she glanced at her watch. "It's been five minutes, and they're still at it. I suppose we should get in there before they kill each other."

"Sounds good," he agreed, grateful for the distraction.

He stood and waited for her before starting up the steps. Pausing on the tread above him, she turned back with a wry smile. "How ironic that the new Barrett in town is turning out to be the voice of reason around this place."

"Funny, I was just thinking the same thing."

Nailing him with what he sincerely hoped was a mock glare, she spun around and continued up the steps. It was good to see she had some fire under that icy veneer, he thought as he followed her. With the challenges she and her family were facing right now, she was going to need all the attitude she could get.

# *Chapter Six*

The rest of Tess's first week at the mill flew by in a whirlwind of paperwork, fielding phone calls and monitoring orders on the website. They came in from all over the country, Canada and a few even originated overseas, which required her to flag them for special shipping arrangements to ensure those items would arrive in time for Christmas. Chelsea had set up an alarm to let Tess know when a new order arrived, and even though it was a pleasant chiming sound, it seemed to interrupt her at the worst possible times.

Then there was the crew. Even with Scott and Jason at the helm, they were an unruly bunch of men's men who were polite enough but clearly didn't view her with the same respect they did Chelsea. After a few days, she'd come to the conclusion that being a Barrett would only get her so far with the locals. The rest was up to her.

All this ran through her head as she drove through town on Saturday morning. As an experienced retail girl, Tess was accustomed to being available on weekends, so the extra workday didn't bother her. Now that the mill was running more smoothly, she was optimistic that today would go well. Still, she was fairly certain this shift was going to be worlds away from the classical music, lattes and scones she used to have for her customers in Beverly Hills.

For one thing, she knew if she brought in fancy treats like that, her rough-around-the-edges cousins and their buddies would laugh themselves hoarse. So she stopped by the bakery and picked up a few dozen assorted donuts and a couple of flaky croissants for herself. She added a to-go tray of steaming coffee and some soothing tea for Chelsea. Everything was so fresh, the aroma made her stomach rumble as she loaded them into the truck and headed for Paul and Chelsea's. Each day, one family member or another stopped by to check on them and bring the expectant parents something yummy to eat. Tess was proud to be chipping in, even if it was only to deliver donuts and coffee.

Seven-thirty was still like the crack of dawn

for her, but she was getting used to the early mornings and long hours that seemed to be a part of life in this blue-collar town. Several people beeped at her, raising their hands in a good-morning salute she returned with a smile. While she didn't know most of them, she thought it was nice of them to acknowledge the new Barrett in town that way. On the LA freeway, she recalled grimly, it was almost unheard of to make it to your destination without someone in a rush cutting you off. Or worse.

When she arrived at her cousin's home, Boyd bounded through the front yard to greet her, his large ears flapping in excitement. Apparently, they were best friends now, and as he wrapped his legs around her waist in a canine hug, she was glad she'd worn jeans.

"Good morning to you, too, handsome," she cooed, ruffling his jowls as she planted a kiss over his droopy eyes.

Accustomed to dealing with more refined personalities, she found his unabashed exuberance a delightful change of pace. Come to think of it, she mused as she crunched through the fallen leaves to the front door, the people around here were the same way. Outgoing and friendly and, like Heath and Fred, ready to lend a hand when needed. It hadn't taken her long to get used to that, and she marked the difference as another in the *pro* column for this sleepy little town.

She knocked softly on the front door and was surprised when Paul opened it almost immediately.

"I smell coffee," he said simply, stepping back to let her inside.

"Molly Harkness insisted I bring you some." His enthusiasm made her smile, and she handed it over. "She said it's your favorite blend."

After a long sip, he let out an appreciative sigh. "It is, but don't tell Gram."

"Don't worry," she assured him with a wink. "Your secret's safe with me. Is Chelsea awake? I've got croissants."

"Oh, bless you," a voice chimed in from the living room. "I'm starving."

As they strolled in Paul reminded his wife, "You just ate an hour ago."

From her lounging position on the sofa, she gave him one of those raised eyebrow looks. "And I'll eat in another hour, too. This is a Barrett I'm growing in here, you know."

"So you keep telling me," he replied with a chuckle.

Tess noticed an antique piano stool in the corner and glanced around. "Where's the piano?"

"I have no idea," Chelsea admitted while she tore apart the tender croissant and popped a piece in her mouth. "I found the stool at an antiques show over in Cambridge and thought it was interesting so I bought it."

Okay. In Tess's world, no one bought anything that didn't match what they already owned, so the eclectic approach to decorating was new to her. Still, the pieces Chelsea had used seemed to complement each other, in a shabby-chic kind of way. "How's the bathroom coming, Paul?"

"It's usable, but there's still some finishing work left. Fortunately, we had a powder room on this floor already so I just had to enlarge it for a step-in shower. I figure it'll come in handy when we're old and creaky."

"I can't wait until the baby comes so you can stop carrying me up and down the stairs," his wife added.

"And here I thought it was romantic."

They traded a loving look, and Tess couldn't help envying them their happiness. Despite their obvious worry over the baby, they had each other to lean on, to help make things a little easier to navigate. Having weathered the loss of her baby and then her fiancé completely on her own, she wished someone had been there to offer her a shoulder to lean on.

Someone like Heath.

Out of nowhere, his name popped into her

mind. At first she didn't understand why, and then she recalled their conversation during the worknight picnic at the mill. How he'd reached out to comfort her over something that had happened months ago, even though they hadn't known each other then. Instinctively, she knew that if she ever found herself in trouble now, he'd be there for her. Not to mention her extended family, who accepted her just as she was, rather than harping on one flaw or another the way her parents and siblings had always done.

That was when it hit her. The problem wasn't with her, the way she'd always assumed. It was with them. Driven by their desire for wealth and status, they discounted anything outside that realm as worthless or a waste of time.

When she'd told him about her plans to come east and help out at the sawmill, her father had stared at her as if they'd never met. What would he think of the upcoming scarecrow contest? she wondered. Then, to her amazement, she realized she couldn't possibly care less. Maybe Heath was right and she had more country in her than she thought. Whatever the reason, she resolved to embrace this new opportunity and make the most of it.

Wherever it might take her, at least this time she was charting her own path instead of following one that had been chosen for her. When it occurred to her that Paul had asked her a question, she dragged her brain away from her meandering thoughts and said, "Sorry, I checked out there for a second. What did you say?"

"I asked how things are going for you at the mill. Chelsea and I have never been gone this long, and I'm sure you've had a few issues out there."

"Meaning your brothers?" When he chuckled, she quickly went on. "They've been great, and so has everyone else. Everyone knows I'm still learning, so they're being patient with me." Most of the time. And when they weren't, she handled the situation with what was rapidly becoming her approach to life in general: humor and a smile. To her delight, not only did people respond better to her now, but she was enjoying her days more, too. They weren't easy, by any means, but she had a much better understanding of the motivational plaque in Chelsea's office: Attitude is everything.

"And production? How far behind are we?"

"We're not. Everything's going fine."

Technically, she was telling the truth. As far as she was concerned, the fact that she'd revamped the schedule to allow for having only one working saw was something Paul didn't need to worry about.

Unfortunately, his wife wasn't so easily fooled. She gave Tess a long, suspicious look but thankfully didn't say anything. Apparently, she shared the family's opinion that Paul was needed much more at home than at the mill. Tess hoped that by the time he returned on Monday, the other two saws would be up and running at full strength, and the temporary slowdown could remain a well-guarded secret.

"Well, I should get going," she said as she stood up. "I promised the crew I'd bring them breakfast, and I don't want them beating me to work." Leaning down, she hugged Chelsea. "Take good care of yourself, now. Your only job is to give that little one as much time as he needs to get ready to come into the world, okay?"

Chelsea's eyes shone with sudden emotion, and she nodded. "Thanks, Tess. I don't know where we'd be without your help. You're a real lifesaver."

Tess couldn't recall ever being referred to that way, and she felt herself getting a little misty, too. Before she gave in to actual tears, she waved good-bye and followed Paul into the foyer. With his hand on the antique glass knob, he gave her a long, somber look. "Before you go, I think there's something you oughta know."

"Really?" His manner was making her very uncomfortable, and she did her best to appear unconcerned. "What's that?"

"You're a terrible liar." His serious expression gave way to a grin. "If you were a puppet, your nose would be longer than when you got here."

Pulling herself up to her full height, she gave him a steely glare. "I have no idea what you're talking about."

That only made him laugh, and after a couple of seconds she joined him. "You're not mad, are you?"

"Are we gonna make our holiday deadlines?"

"Yes. Everyone said they'd donate overtime if that's what it takes to get all the work done."

"Then it sounds to me like the business is in good hands," he said with a warm smile. "Great job."

Unaccustomed to receiving praise for anything other than her fashion sense, Tess appreciated the pat on the back more than she could say. But to Paul, she simply said, "Thanks."

A bark sounded out front, and they looked out to find Boyd in the back of the old mill truck, eagerly wagging his tail.

"I think he wants to come with me," she commented with another laugh.

"Would it be too much for you to take him with you? Daisy doesn't mind lying on the couch with Chelsea all day, but he's going bonkers cooped up in the house. He never wanders far from the mill, but he loves running around in the woods and up to Scott and Jenna's place."

"No problem," she blurted without a second thought. She'd never had a pet, and even though he wasn't hers, the concept of bringing the big bloodhound to work with her had a nice, homey appeal.

"His food's in a bin in the office, and he'll let you know when he wants to go out," Paul said as he walked her to the truck. "You're not having any more trouble with this old beast, are you?"

"Not since Heath worked on it last. In fact, I was hoping it would be okay for me to keep using it."

"You mean, even after Gram's car is fixed?" When she nodded, he gave her a confused look. "Why?"

She ran her hand over the rough hood, wondering if she was losing her mind. Normally, she wasn't the sort of girl to get all mushy over a car, but this one was different somehow. "It's grown on me, I guess. Now that I've got the hang of the transmission and found an AM station I like, it's kind of fun to drive."

"Fine by me. It's not like anyone's lining up to take it off your hands."

"Not quite."

Laughing, he said, "Thanks so much for letting Boyd tag along. You're gonna make his day."

"It'll be nice to have some company in the office. You ready to go, handsome?" she asked, reaching over the side of the cargo area to pat his head. Woofing, he rubbed his cheek against her hand as if he actually understood her.

She climbed into the cab and pulled away from the house, taking the curve gently to avoid upsetting the dog's balance. For his part, he stood at the front of the truck bed, his head dangling just behind where she sat as he gulped in the cool morning breeze. If only her LA friends could see her now, she thought with a grin. They'd think she'd completely lost her marbles.

When she drove past Mill Office Supply, she noticed Paige by the old-fashioned lamppost out front, surrounded by bales of straw. Her curiosity piqued, Tess pulled up to the curb and waved at the clerk through the open passenger window. "Whatcha doin'?"

"Cogitating, as my grandpa Ike would say. I'm in charge of our scarecrow display this year, and I've got no idea where to start."

Tess laughed, happy to discover she wasn't the only one struggling with her unusual assignment. "Me, too. Except I'm not even at the cogitating phase yet. It got sprung on me the other night, and I didn't have the brainpower left to do much more than nod."

"Oh, you're a Barrett," Paige reminded her confidently. "You'll do great."

Tess still wasn't entirely certain what being a Barrett meant to the folks around here, but anytime someone mentioned it, they seemed to have something good to say about her family. That they'd begun including her in that positive light made her feel more at home every day. "I forgot to ask the boys about the rules. Is there some kind of theme we have to follow?"

"No, but what a great idea! I'll bring it up at this month's town meeting so we can add it for next year."

Seriously? Tess wondered silently. A town meeting? In her experience, those were reserved for campaign season, when candidates were anxious to impress voters with how in touch they were with the needs and concerns of regular people. For some reason, the notion of attending a less contrived version appealed to her, and she asked, "Can anyone go to those?"

"Sure. As long as you behave yourself," Paige added with a grin. "A couple months ago, Grandpa got tossed for laughing at a proposal he thought was completely ridiculous. To be fair he was probably right, but our mayor, Bruce Harkness, brought it up, and he didn't take kindly to being ridiculed in front of everyone."

Tess was officially running late, and she tried to tamp down her inquisitiveness so she could get going. Really, she did, but in the end she couldn't resist asking, "What was the idea?"

Paige came over and rested her arms across the window ledge. The gesture made Tess think of Heath, and she firmly put the image of him out of her mind. Considering the mess her personal life was currently in, she knew the less she thought about the friendly mechanic, the better.

"Bruce wanted to build a replica of the mill in the town square, as part of a new playground."

"Well, that's not so crazy."

"Complete with a creek and working waterwheel," Paige went on.

Tess glanced down the street and then back

to the chatty young woman. "The creek doesn't run through town."

"Exactly. Grandpa didn't have a problem with the scaled-down sawmill, but he thought it was nuts to dig out a channel that would have to constantly be supplied with water when God laid down a perfectly good creek a couple miles away."

Tess understood that, but she couldn't help thinking the idea had merit. "How much did Bruce think something like that would cost?"

"More than we can spare right now. With the economy the way it is, most folks around here are just getting by, and the town funds shrink a little more every year. We've got all we can do to keep up the roads and sidewalks, and lately even those projects are getting delayed."

Paige couldn't be more than twenty-five, Tess estimated. Her grasp of local issues and her eloquent way of stating them was impressive, to say the least. "It sounds to me like you could run for office yourself."

"Don't think I haven't considered it. But I'm too young—" holding up two fingers, she ticked off one "—and a woman, besides." She ticked off the other. "It'll never happen."

One thing LA and Barrett's Mill had in common, Tess groused. No matter how open-minded they claimed to be, too often people still clung to the traditional ways of doing things. That meant young women like Paige and her, with drive and fresh ideas, got left on the sidelines while others plodded along the same, unimaginative path they always had. And where did that get you? Absolutely nowhere.

"Someday, you'll make it happen," she predicted, pleased when her new friend smiled brightly. "In the meantime, just make the best scarecrow you can. That's the only way you're going to beat us."

Paige laughed. "In your dreams, Cali girl. I've been doing this since I was five, and you're the greenest greenhorn in town. You and your ratty straw man don't stand a chance."

"You never know," Tess shot back with a grin. "I might come up with something that knocks everyone's socks off."

Clearly unfazed, Paige grinned back. "I guess we'll know soon enough. If you're still interested, the town meeting is always the last Thursday of the month at seven. We meet in the fellowship hall at the Crossroads Church, and if you want a seat, you should get there about fifteen minutes early."

Tess couldn't believe that was actually necessary, but she didn't want to question it and create the impression that she was a rude outsider. "Thanks. If I finish work in time, I'll come check it out."

"Fabulous. It'd be nice to have another woman there under the age of sixty. Know what I mean?"

Tess responded with a smile and waved as she pulled out of the zone designated for short-term parking. The sun was rising in the eastern sky, and she admired the view over the tops of the centuries-old trees that stood alongside Main Street like guardians watching over the town. Hazy purple merged with pink and gold, spreading across the horizon in layered colors softened by mist rolling up out of the valley that surrounded her.

When she'd been here a month ago, the fields and forests had seemed to merge together in a lush, deep green that went on forever. Now that color was giving way to a range of golds and reds like nothing she'd ever seen in California. From vivid to pale, some of them were such a unique hue she couldn't identify them except to say that they were incredible.

Just one more thing to appreciate here, she thought, carefully slowing and double-checking for other cars before turning onto Mill Road. During her commute the last few days, she hadn't come across a single car. Because of that, she found it odd that she'd managed to literally run into Heath that first morning. If Tess hadn't known better, she would have suspected her grandmother of somehow arranging their dramatic meeting. Then again, she thought with a smile, if anyone was capable of it, it would be Gram.

When she reached the end of the lane, she was surprised to find Heath's mini–monster truck parked next to half a dozen less flashy pickups. As she got out, Boyd leaped from the truck and dashed off in pursuit of something rustling in the nearby hedgerow. What would it be like, she wondered, to be able to run off on a whim like that? While she was a lifelong city girl, the more time she spent out in the woods, the more she wanted to explore the area around the mill and discover what made it so special that her cousins were fighting to keep it in the family.

"Something wrong?"

Hearing Heath's voice behind her, she turned to find him standing on the porch, wiping grease from his hands. It seemed to be a frequent thing for him, and she knew that image of him would stay with her long after she left town. Where she came from, his faded blue T-shirt and well-loved jeans would have been considered stylish and priced accordingly. But she knew his had been weathered by plenty of tough wear and washing, which suited his hands-on lifestyle perfectly.

Despite her promise to focus solely on righting herself while she was in Barrett's Mill, she couldn't deny that she'd grown fond of the rugged mechanic with the generous heart. Smiling, she said, "I was just wishing I could follow Boyd and find out what's so fascinating out there."

"Why can't you?"

"First of all, I've got breakfast for the crew." She opened the passenger door and lifted out the stack of goodies she'd bought in town. "And after that, I really need to figure out how those spreadsheets of Chelsea's work. If I get too far behind, I'll never catch up."

As she made her way up the steps, Heath opened the door for her and chuckled. "Well, I know food's important, but it seems to me like the computer stuff could wait half an hour."

"Everyone's working so hard, I'd hate to make it look like I'm slacking off," she confided quietly.

Even though the sliding door was closed, she could still hear the one functioning saw going, and behind it the steady grinding noise of the lathe. She'd seen it in motion, but it still amazed her that anyone could use such a basic piece of equipment to turn a rectangular piece of wood into a tapered table leg or a spindle for the back of one of their handcrafted rocking chairs. In her world, when you wanted furniture, you went to a store and bought what you needed without much thought for how it came to be made.

Here, she'd seen old-fashioned craftsmanship that blew factory-made pieces out of the water. If only more people knew about the fine pieces they produced here, she mused, Barrett's Mill Furniture would be solidly in the black for years to come. And, if she could devise a strategy for making that happen, she'd have the satisfaction of knowing she'd made a valuable contribution to the future of her family and many others, besides.

"Uh-oh," Heath commented with another chuckle. "That's a troublemaker look if ever I saw one. What's going through that head of yours?"

"Just cogitating."

For some reason, he groaned. "Oh, man, you've been talking to Paige Donaldson, haven't you?"

"You make that sound like it's a bad thing," Tess shot back with a glare. "She and I really hit it off, and I think she's fabulous."

"That's not a surprise." Shaking his head with honest male bewilderment, he went on.

"You're like two peas in a pod. Easy on the eyes and tough on the nerves."

No one had ever spoken to her that way. Oh, she'd gotten plenty of backhanded compliments over the years, but none had come with the crooked grin she was getting from him now. This country boy had a knack for throwing her off balance, and it didn't even seem like he had to try all that hard. Instinct told her that meant something, but she wasn't about to ponder it now.

"Whatever." Setting out the bakery boxes she'd brought, she punched the buttons to start the dual coffeemaker and spun to leave. She was wearing her lowest heels, but the pad got caught in the crack between two old floorboards, and she stumbled. Before she knew what was happening, she found herself in Heath's arms. Again.

"This feels familiar," he teased, grasping her shoulders to steady her before he stepped away. "You really need to get some more practical shoes."

Normally, the slip and unwanted advice would have only soured her mood further. But to her astonishment, she found herself laughing instead. "Yeah, I know. Maybe Jenna will help me pick out some new clothes at the mall."

"You want fashion help from Mrs. Overalls and Sneakers?"

"Good point." Seeing an opportunity to needle him, she said, "Paige dresses well. It'd be fun to shop with her and get to know her better."

"Thanks for the warning," he grumbled as he turned to go.

"Heath?" When he looked back, she smiled. "Thanks for catching me."

"Anytime, magpie."

He flashed her the kind of grin that had probably weakened a few knees over the years and headed back to the production area. Because she simply couldn't help it, Tess allowed herself a moment to admire him as he strolled away. He moved with a fluid power born of the quiet confidence he carried with him everywhere he went. It struck her that his strength of character came from meeting challenges head-on and winning. His self-assuredness wasn't an act, something he projected with the intent of impressing anyone. That was simply who he was, and she suspected he'd never even considered trying to be anyone else.

One day Tess wanted to feel that kind of poise herself.

Now that she'd put the dizzying orbit of Avery's social circle behind her, she realized it had taken a lot from her and given nothing in return. She'd exhausted herself trying to fit into that group, only to find that in the end she didn't have what it took.

By contrast, the moment she'd arrived in Barrett's Mill for Scott and Jenna's wedding, she'd felt more welcome than she had in her entire life. That was why she'd come back, she recognized as she walked across the lobby to boot up her computer and get started. As good as she felt about helping her family during a difficult time, they were doing even more for her. They treated her with respect, accepting her for who she was rather than attempting to mold her into something else entirely. Through their generosity they'd given her something no one could buy, no matter how much money they had.

Hope.

Heath was getting a real education in turn-of-the-century technology. The hands-on kind, he added silently while he strained to loosen what was left of a bolt that had busted off in place and was preventing him from replacing what looked like a hand-forged metal strut. Paul's mind was understandably elsewhere these days, so Heath had volunteered to do a thorough inspection of the antiquated machinery that powered the waterwheel. Within ten seconds, he'd keyed in on a section that wobbled so much, he was afraid it would fly off any day now.

Dangling from the underside of the mill house was tough on his still-mending shoulder, and he rubbed it to ease the strain. When that didn't help, he leaned back against the framing timber, closing his eyes while he let the tight muscles relax.

"Are you okay?"

He opened his eyes to find Tess staring down at him, a bottle of water in one hand and an anxious look on her face. He regretted the worry clouding those beautiful eyes, and he smiled to ease her concern. "Just taking a break."

She tilted her head as if she didn't quite believe that but to his surprise, she didn't call him on it. "You don't look very comfortable hanging that way."

"It's not an easy position to get in. If I take a break, I have to climb down again, and I'm not keen on doing it more than once. I'll be done soon enough. I think," he added wryly.

"I thought you might be thirsty."

After their earlier exchange, her thoughtful gesture was a pleasant surprise. This woman had more twists and turns than a mountain road, and he caught himself wondering how many more there might be. Since that was something he had no intention of finding out, he pushed the question aside. "I am, thanks. Toss it down and I'll catch it."

Unfortunately, her throw went astray, and he had to dart his bad arm out to keep the bottle from falling into the creek below. Wincing, he let out an unconscious grunt that made her gasp.

"Oh, Heath, I'm sorry! I'll go get Scott."

"No!" The whip in his voice stopped her cold, and he regretted his harsh reaction to her offer. "Sorry, I didn't mean to yell at you. I'm fine, just a little sore from hanging under here like this."

"You're not fine," she informed him primly. "You can lie to me, but you should be honest with yourself."

"That sounds familiar," he joked.

"You should take your own advice. You should also come up here and have something to eat. It's past lunchtime."

Squinting up at her, he grinned. "You're starting to sound like your grandmother."

"That's the nicest thing anyone's ever said to me," she replied, beaming down at him. "Now, get up here. I'm sure one of the boys will help you finish that up later."

"Yes, ma'am."

While Heath pulled himself up and clambered over the railing, he noticed she didn't turn and go back inside but waited for him on the walkway. Watching over him protectively, she reached out to steady him as he cautiously lowered himself down to the weathered planks. Small as she was, there wasn't much she could've done for him if he lost his balance, but he appreciated her thoughtful gesture all the same.

"Safe and sound," he assured her, coiling his well-used rappelling gear into a neat bundle he slung over his right shoulder. The left one was still barking, and he decided to give the strenuous stuff a rest for now.

"You looked right at home down there," she commented as they made their way into the mill house. "Did you used to do a lot of that kind of thing?"

"Yeah. That was one of the skills that got me my oil rig job." The job that had nearly cost him his life, he recalled grimly. Shoving the uncharacteristic negativity back where it belonged, he tapped into some more pleasant memories. "On the weekends a bunch of us would go into the mountains to camp and go climbing. It was tough, but the views from the top of those peaks made it all worthwhile."

"I can only imagine."

In the lobby Heath glanced over the Dutch door into the office. Stunned by what he saw, he had to look again to be sure his eyes weren't deceiving him. They weren't, and he whistled in amazement. "It looks great in there. What'd you do—burn everything?"

"Filing, filing and more filing," she replied with a laugh. "I've spent most of the week logging things in and moving them from the 'to-do' pile to the 'done' pile. It was tedious and boring, but I finally got everything caught up and put away."

Something in her tone alerted him that things weren't as simple as that, and he frowned. "And?"

She studied him for a few moments, and he got the distinct impression she was trying to decide if she could trust him with whatever she had to say. Looking over her shoulder, she came back to him and murmured, "Not here."

"How 'bout out there?" he asked, nodding out the side window toward the woods. "I could use a walk, anyway."

"What about your lunch?"

Reaching over the door, he plucked an old wool blanket off the chair where Daisy liked to nap and draped it over his shoulder. "We'll call it a picnic. I'll even share my sandwich with you."

"Gram packed me some leftovers. I just didn't have the stomach for them earlier."

Must be bad, he thought while Tess got her own lunch from the small office fridge. When they had everything, he followed her down the porch steps and out toward the trail Boyd had worn through the undergrowth from the sawmill to Scott and Jenna's place upstream.

Figuring she needed this field trip more than he did, Heath let Tess lead the way and the conversation. She chattered on about clerical issues he had little understanding of, but they seemed important to her, so he did his best to keep up with what she was telling him. As they strolled alongside Sterling Creek, she seemed to relax a bit more with each step, and he was glad to see the fresh air seemed to be making her feel better.

For his part, he'd taken this path many times over the years, but it never failed to impress him. With some of their leaves already gone, the branches overhead let plenty of sunlight through, and it played over the bubbling water like a spotlight. He saw a flash of minnows under the surface and assessed the progress a family of beavers had made on their small dam since the last time he was out here.

When he was growing up, he'd often explored the acres of forest surrounding the mill with Will Barrett and his grandsons. Mostly a way to get them out from underfoot while people were trying to work, Will also used those hikes to teach them how to identify various trees and critters they shared the property with.

In his memory, he could still hear the old woodsman's voice. *Give the wild things their space, and they'll do the same for you.*

When Heath shared that memory with Tess, she gave him a sad smile. "Every time someone mentions Granddad, I love him more. I wish so much that I could've met him."

"Me, too. Whenever I'm here, I get the feeling he's still around, keeping an eye on the place." He offered her a reassuring smile. "I'm sure he's real proud of you."

She gave him a long, doubtful look. "You honestly believe he's up there somewhere—" she arced her hand through the air "—watching over all of us?"

"Yeah, I do."

"What makes you so sure?"

"Faith means believing in something just because you do," he explained gently, hoping to make her understand. "You must've felt that way about something in your life at one point or another."

After a moment she gave him a sour look.

"Yes, and look where it got me. Dis-engaged and unemployed."

"You're too young to be that cynical."

"And too old to be naive," she spat back. "So where does that leave me?"

Clearly frustrated, she stared off into the distance, and he assumed her question was intended to hang in the air, unanswered. He sent up a quick prayer for this bitter, disillusioned young woman who'd lost so much and seemed to have no idea where she was going next. Not long ago he'd experienced something very similar, and he understood all too well how demoralizing it could be.

Eager to change the subject, he said, "I finished with Olivia's car this morning. Fred's dropping it off on his way home."

"That's nice of him."

"Nice, nothing," he corrected her with a grin. "Everyone knows she bakes on Saturdays, and he's probably hoping to get himself something good to eat."

That made her laugh, and he congratulated himself on lightening her mood a bit. She was edgier than usual, and while he was anxious to learn what was bugging her, he didn't want to push her to talk. He hated it when folks did that to him, and he wasn't about to make that mistake with Tess.

"Oh, look," she murmured, stopping to point out a red fox edging from the woods to get a drink. When another appeared, she sighed quietly. "They're so beautiful."

"Yeah, they are." They watched the animals until they were finished drinking and trotted back in the same direction they'd come from. Figuring this was as good a place as any, Heath flung the blanket out and motioned to her. "After you."

She rewarded him with a bright smile that rivaled the sunshine. "You have to be the sweetest guy I've ever met. After I just about bit your head off, too."

"I hate to break this to you, darlin'," he said with a laugh, "but you don't scare me. My rig boss in Alaska was way meaner than you."

"It works with everyone else," she complained with a fairly convincing pout.

"I guess I'm not like them."

Those keen eyes studied him for a long moment, and she slowly nodded. "I guess you're right."

Once seated, they both spread out their lunches on the blanket in an unspoken agreement to share. Olivia's meat loaf complemented his roast beef sandwich perfectly, and they combined the fruit they'd brought into a nice salad. Leaning back on his elbows, he stretched out his legs and dropped his head back to watch a bank of fluffy clouds drifting through the sky. "Sure beats eating in the back room with the crew."

"Do you mean the food or the company?"

Rolling his head to look over at her, he grinned. "Both."

"Flattery will get you nowhere with me, country boy," she warned, though the sudden blush on her cheeks said otherwise. "But you get an A for effort."

"No effort involved. Just callin' it like I see it."

That made her laugh, which was a real achievement considering the foul mood she'd been in earlier. "The girls around here must fall all over themselves trying to get your attention."

"Nah. I'm just Heath, the goofball they all grew up with."

"That's not what the girls around here say," she informed him as she popped a melon ball in her mouth. "I heard you were quite the ladies' man."

Her tone was light, but in her eyes he saw something quite different. He got the feeling she was testing him, but he couldn't for the life of him figure out why. "That was a long time ago. I'm not looking for that anymore."

"Because of your accident?" When he nodded, she frowned. "It changed a lot of things for you, didn't it?"

"If it didn't, I'd get my head examined. Something like that makes you take a good look at yourself, and when you do that, you find some stuff you like and some you don't." She didn't say anything, but he could see he had her full attention. Sensing an opportunity to make a point with her, he forged ahead. "We can't change what happened to us in the past, but the future is wide open. We can make that better if we want."

She absorbed that while picking through the salad for more watermelon. "What do you see in your future?"

"A wife who thinks I hung the moon, and a bunch of kids who think I'm the greatest dad ever."

"Really?" Tess asked incredulously. "That's all?"

Sadly, her response didn't surprise him, and he met it with as much understanding as he could. "To me, that's everything."

After chewing for a few moments, she said, "I guess it's nice to know what you want."

"Yeah, it is." She'd pulled back from him, and he decided it was time to shift to a less personal subject. "So, what did you wanna tell me before?"

Sighing, she swallowed some of her water. "The mill's not doing well."

"What else is new?"

"I mean, really not well. Every number I come up with is red, and Chelsea's income projections are horrible. Things tick up at the holidays, but once that work goes away, things nosedive in a hurry. If we don't come up with something new to entice people to buy their furniture from us, we'll hardly be able to make our loan payments, much less pay everyone. Why on earth are you smiling?" she demanded angrily.

"You keep saying *we*. Like you consider yourself part of the crew now."

"Well, I—" she began, obviously caught off guard by his assessment. A few seconds later, she gave him a slowly dawning smile. "I suppose I do feel that way, even though I haven't been here very long. Weird, huh?"

"Cool," he corrected her with an encouraging grin. "Anyway, sounds to me like things are the same with the business as they've always been. It's not a gold mine, y'know."

"We either have to increase our revenue or cut expenses somehow. It's great that we don't use a ton of electricity because of the waterwheel, but the price we're paying for our raw materials is ridiculous."

"When they were in Oregon, Paul and Jason worked for the logging outfit that supplies the reclaimed timber," Heath explained. "Building custom pieces from those old trees is part of what makes Barrett's Mill Furniture unique."

"They could use other wood for some projects. Cutting that cost in half would go a long way toward improving the bottom line."

"This place isn't about the bottom line. It's about tradition. Since it opened, this mill has been the Barretts' legacy. Your legacy," he added, hoping to appeal to her growing fondness for the family she'd only begun getting to know.

"If everyone's out of a job, they won't care very much about tradition," she grumbled.

He understood her stance on this particular angle of the problem. Losing her position at the boutique she liked so much had left her pride bruised, and she was still recovering from the added impact of her fiancé's betrayal. Because he could relate to having everything you relied on yanked out from under you, he decided it was best to give her a break on this one.

"Paul will come up with something," he promised her with a reassuring smile. "He always does."

"What if this time he can't? Then what?"

"Then we'll boot him out and stage a coup," he suggested, adding a villainous cackle. "I'll take over the equipment, you put a block on the computers. No one could do a thing to stop us."

His outrageous suggestion had the intended effect, and mischief twinkled in her eyes. "And then?"

"You're the brains, sweetheart," he told her with a wink. "I'm just the muscle."

Laughing, she held up her water, and they tapped their bottles to seal their arrangement. Her concerns hadn't gone away, of course, but Heath was confident that if they all put their heads together, they'd be able to work their way out of the red.

Failure simply wasn't an option for the Barretts. Because as far as he knew, there was no Plan B.

# Chapter Seven

What was that incredible smell?

Cracking one eye open, Tess peeked at the vintage alarm clock on her bedside table and saw it was nearly nine on Sunday morning. Outside her window, sunlight was trying to make its way through the overlying clouds, while a neighbor's dog barked at whatever had caught his attention. Someone shouted for him to knock it off, and the sound trailed off into a compliant whimper. Shortly after that, though, he started up again, and she heard the slam of a screen door before everything went quiet again.

Considering the long, challenging week she'd had at the mill, she'd anticipated sleeping until noon and enjoying a peaceful breakfast in her grandmother's kitchen. When she finally identified the aroma drifting upstairs as roast beef, Tess suspected her plan was about to be thwarted by one of Gram's famous Barrett family gatherings. Jenna had told her about them, and Tess was looking forward to experiencing one for herself. She just wasn't figuring it would be today.

More curious than disappointed, she pulled on her robe and padded down the hallway in her bare feet. The upper floor of the old farmhouse housed five bedrooms, a testament to several generations of large families. Granddad had grown up here, she recalled as she peered into the spare room across from hers. Then he and Gram had raised their own family, and now the place stood mostly empty.

Not lonely, though, she thought with a smile as she headed down the front stairs. The comfortable old house echoed with memories, and if she used her imagination, she could imagine her cousins sliding down the mahogany banister to the ground floor. Racing, probably.

Had her father done that as a child? she wondered, running a hand down the polished railing and over the hand-carved newel post. She couldn't picture him being mischievous and carefree, but she'd only known him as an adult, and a detached one at that. When he'd left his homespun roots behind to make his fortune, had he lost a part of himself that he couldn't get back?

"Good morning, Tessie," Gram sang when she entered the kitchen. "Sleep well?"

"Like a rock. You've been busy in here," she added, nodding at what looked like preparations for an army feast. "What's up?"

"It's Sunday."

The offhanded reply stunned Tess, who saw her parents rarely and only connected with her older siblings when they put in an appearance at her mother's obligatory holiday party. "You have a family dinner here every Sunday?"

"Of course. Cooking is like any other skill… use it or lose it."

That phrase sounded hilarious coming from a petite eighty-year-old woman, and Tess couldn't keep back a laugh. "That makes sense, I guess. Can I do anything to help?"

"The girls and I agreed to bring everything to Paul and Chelsea's after church. If you could bring in those covered serving dishes from the pantry, that would be nice."

"Are you sure Chelsea's up for so much company?"

"Paul all but begged us to come over and visit for a while. Chelsea's feeling cooped up and thinks she's missing all the goings-on around town." Gram paused with a wistful look. "I can relate to that. When your grand-dad was so sick, I kept luring folks over here to make sure he didn't feel too isolated. Some-times people think you want peace and quiet when you're fighting so hard, but what he re-ally wanted was to feel like he was still part of things. Chelsea needs that as much as rest right now, so we're making sure she gets it."

"I think it's a wonderful idea." Tess ap-proved wholeheartedly. It certainly beat curl-ing up in a ball and waiting for the situation to improve on its own. Which she knew from personal experience. When she was finished bringing in the travel dishes, she asked, "Any-thing else?"

Gram glanced up at the clock. "That's it for now. If I don't get going, I'll be late for church."

She was already dressed in nice clothes, so Tess was confused. "It's just up the street. Now that your car's back, it should take you less than a minute."

"Oh, I don't drive to church. I walk."

That didn't seem wise to Tess, and she searched for a diplomatic way to say so. "The weather app on my phone says it's kind of chilly outside."

"My trip to the backyard tells me it's a good day for a sweater, but I'll be fine."

"What if it rains?"

Cocking her head, Gram gave her a knowing look. "Are you trying to say you think I'm too old to walk half a mile through town?"

"Umm…"

"It's sweet of you to worry, dear," Gram said, gently patting her cheek, "but there's really no need. On the way, I always run into the Morgans and Donaldsons and plenty of other folks heading in the same direction. They'll keep an eye on me, if that makes you feel better."

Tess noticed her very diplomatic grandmother hadn't even hinted that they might walk to church together. The message was clear: if Tess wanted to come along, that was fine. If not, Gram would accept that decision, too. For someone who'd spent a lifetime chafing against other people's expectations of her, that kind of tolerance was liberating.

Then one of the names Gram had mentioned registered more clearly. "You said Donaldson. Do you mean Paige's grandparents?"

"That's right, I forgot you girls met the other day. Paige got her mother's looks, bless her, but inherited Ike's grit. He and Lila stood up for us at our wedding, and we did the same for them."

"I like Paige," Tess commented, her wavering attitude about church suddenly gone. "And I wouldn't mind meeting them."

Gram beamed her approval. "I think they'd enjoy that, too. I'll wait while you get ready."

"Thanks."

In the center of the table, there was a plate stacked with blueberry muffins, and she grabbed one on her way by. The enormous muffin was still warm, and she hummed her opinion as the first bite all but melted in her mouth. She sincerely doubted there was a high-end bakery anywhere on the planet that could compete with Gram's cooking.

After a quick shower, she pulled on a flowery dress and braided her damp hair so it hung over one shoulder. A quick survey of her shoes reminded her that she still needed to buy some practical footwear, and she made a mental note to invite Paige on a shopping expedition that afternoon. Then she rustled through her still-packed suitcases for a light sweater and hurried downstairs.

Gram gave her a once-over and a nod of approval. "Very pretty."

"Just trying to keep up with you."

"Oh, you," she chided, waving off the compliment with a laugh. "You're just like your cousins, flattering an old lady to get on my good side."

"I didn't think you had a bad side."

As they stood there smiling at each other,

Tess was struck by the realization that this was yet another in a long line of pleasant moments she'd had recently. That they'd all taken place in Barrett's Mill couldn't be a coincidence, she decided as they linked arms and walked out the front door together.

Outside they turned and headed up the sidewalk toward the Crossroads Church. Built not long after the mill, the simple white chapel stood at the head of Main Street, like a beacon calling people in to worship. On the way she met Ike and Lila, along with Rachel McCarron and her toddling daughter, Eva.

Farther up, they were joined by Helen and Fred Morgan, who made the introductions for Tess and then leaned in to murmur, "How're things going these days?"

Smiling, she whispered, "Much better, thanks to Heath."

"If that changes, you'll let me know?"

"I will. Thank you."

He winked at her and then dropped back into step beside his wife, who'd been so busy chatting with Gram and Lila she apparently hadn't noticed his absence.

"Mama, bird," Eva piped up in an adorable voice, pointing to a bright yellow finch sitting on a garden post.

Looking over, Rachel hunkered down and

said, "That's right, Eva bean. What does a bird say?"

"Cheep, cheep!"

"Right again." She rewarded the little girl with a hug. "Good for you."

Their sweet exchange made Tess smile, and she felt a twinge of longing. If things had gone right for her, she'd have her own little one now. Someone who gazed up at her with unabashed adoration the way Eva was doing with Rachel. Someone who would treasure her for no reason other than the fact that she was mommy.

Someday, Tess promised herself, she'd feel that kind of joy. And once she did, she'd make sure her child would never, ever question her love. She'd learned firsthand that was the greatest gift a parent could possibly give their children. Sadly, her own mother and father had never understood how precious it was, or if they had they hadn't known how to express those feelings to her. In her darker moments, she doubted they ever would.

Of course, motherhood was on indeterminate hold right now, she admitted with a mental sigh. She'd wasted more than a year with Avery, and varying amounts of time with the men that had come before him. Like her mother, she seemed to have an inborn knack for picking the wrong guys. The question was, how did she go about finding the right one?

"Now, that's an awful serious look for such a nice morning."

Heath's now-familiar drawl put a merciful end to her brooding, and Tess was pleasantly surprised by the change from his everyday appearance. His usual look had a rugged kind of charm to it, but today's gray trousers and crisp white shirt set off his outdoorsy features very nicely. She'd never tell him that, of course. She doubted his male ego needed any boosting from her.

"Sorry," she said. "Just thinking."

"You seem to do a lot o' that," he commented, grinning as he nodded to Gram. "Does it really get you anywhere?"

He had a point there, and she couldn't help laughing. "In trouble, mostly. Where did you come from, anyway?"

"My parents' house is around the corner on Railroad Avenue. They're off exploring the lower forty-eight in their RV, so I'm crashing there for now."

"Are they on a vacation or have they become permanent gypsies?"

"They'll be home for Thanksgiving," he replied, lifting a hand to acknowledge his boss.

"I've got a lead on my own place, and I'm hoping to get all the money stuff lined up soon."

It must be nice to have a plan, she thought enviously. Pushing the negativity aside, she asked, "Is something wrong with your truck?"

"No. I always walk to church with Olivia." Understanding dawned, and he chuckled. "She didn't tell you that, did she?"

"Silly me," Gram chimed in. "It must've slipped my mind."

"Uh-huh. Didn't your granddaughter tell you we're just friends?"

"Repeatedly," she retorted with a sour look.

"Then why don't you believe me?" Tess demanded in exasperation. Apparently, matchmaking was a common hobby in this close-knit little town. While she appreciated the effort the hens were making on her behalf, she wished they'd leave her be.

"I do believe you, dear. I just don't think you're seeing the big picture."

"Which is what?"

"I think it's best to let you discover that on your own," she responded cryptically before striding ahead a few steps to resume her chat with Helen.

The two of them put their heads together, whispering like a couple of teenage girls sharing a secret. When they started giggling, Tess let out an exasperated sigh. "I love her, but sometimes she drives me bonkers."

"Southern women," Heath added with a wide grin as they reached the church. "Gotta love 'em."

Motioning her up the steps ahead of him, he took his time moving through the crowd in the entryway, introducing her to anyone she hadn't already met. By the time they reached their seats, she felt like she'd met the entire population of Barrett's Mill in a five-minute whirl.

"I'm never going to remember all those names," she muttered, taking a hymnal from the pile at the end of the pew.

"Don't worry about it. If you draw a blank on someone, just call 'em *honey*. My mom's got a terrible memory for faces, and she's done that for so long, it's her nickname."

"Honey Weatherby," Tess said, adding a little smile. "That's kind of cute."

"Suits her right down to the ground, as Dad would say."

Tess eyed the tall mechanic with fresh perspective. Her relationship with her own mother and father was dicey, at best. As he continued talking about his parents and their RV adventures, it became obvious that the fondness went both ways.

Like the Barretts.

That warmth totally explained why she'd fit into the Virginia clan so seamlessly. They had what she'd been searching for, and they were more than willing to include her in it.

While she was pondering that, the organist played the opening chords of the first hymn, and Tess absently stood, grateful she'd already opened her book to the right page. A quick glance at Heath, however, showed her that he was watching her with more than mild concern. When he mouthed *Okay?*, she nodded. He smiled down at her, and for the first time she returned the gesture without worrying how it might be perceived. They liked each other, she reasoned. There wasn't any harm in that.

When they finished singing and sat down, she prepared herself for a long-winded, boring lecture about how she should be living her life. To her astonishment, Pastor Griggs came down from the low stage and stood at the head of the aisle. Winging a fatherly look around, he said, "Good morning, everyone."

The congregation replied, and Tess quickly followed along. He made a few announcements, including a not-so-subtle pitch for the upcoming Harvest Festival. "I'm looking forward to seeing what you creative folks have come up with for the displays this year. Since my wife volunteered me to judge, I wanted to let the contestants know I'm open to any and all attempts at bribery as long as they involve something covered in frosting or whipped cream."

Everyone laughed, and Tess found herself warming to the friendly pastor. While he gave a sermon about fresh starts, he struck her as more of an uncle giving them sage advice than a leader giving them orders from on high. He roamed through the chapel, never gazing at her in particular but somehow making her feel as if he'd noticed her and was glad to see her there. Because of her recent experiences, Tess found herself drawn to what he had to say.

"Life often takes us on a journey we didn't anticipate making," he said at one point. "But we need to try to remember that just because we didn't consciously choose it, doesn't mean it's bad. God sees the big picture, and He'll guide us through the wilderness if we trust Him to do it. That kind of faith is difficult for some of us, but if we continue following that path, eventually we'll find ourselves where He means for us to be."

The pastor went on from there, but that last line hit Tess so hard, she actually lost her breath. Sitting here in this quaint little chapel, she finally understood why she'd felt so lost for so long.

All this time she'd been heading in the wrong direction, away from the things that were most important to her. Now that she'd been given a chance to alter her course, where should she go from here?

Something was definitely up with Tess.

Heath had managed to mostly pay attention to the sermon while keeping a casual eye on her. Seeing the variety of emotions playing across her face was more interesting than worrisome, and he couldn't help wondering what was going through that quick mind of hers.

Wearing a dress dotted with blue flowers and a crocheted white sweater, she'd never looked prettier than she did today. Her usual outfits were expertly tailored to cut just the right stylish figure for a workday in LA. Today she looked like she was geared up for a picnic instead of a corporate takeover. While she probably wouldn't appreciate hearing his opinion, he liked the difference. Maybe just a little too much.

While he was wrestling with those very confusing thoughts, a flurry of activity on the other side of the aisle caught his eye. A blond man in a suit was hugging Paige Donaldson, and she was obviously delighted to see him. When Olivia and another elderly woman shifted around to let him sit next to Paige, Heath assumed the two grandmotherly ladies were doing some Sunday morning matchmaking.

Nudging Tess, he discreetly pointed out the little drama unfolding one row back. "I thought she had her hands full with us."

"Apparently she can multitask," Tess commented in a tone laced with fondness. "Never underestimate a Barrett with an agenda."

Focusing his attention back on her, he grinned. "Is that a warning or a threat?"

She didn't answer him, but something like a challenge flared in her eyes. It was a good thing they'd agreed to remain friends, he mused as the organist started up again and everyone stood to sing the final hymn.

Tess Barrett was by far the most fascinating woman he'd ever met. She was also the most complicated, and it would take someone much smarter than him to solve that beautiful, bewildering puzzle. The man brave enough to take that on and allow himself to fall in love with her would definitely have his work cut out for him.

When the service was over, everyone lingered for the customary good-byes and plan-making. As much as he enjoyed Pastor Griggs's commonsense approach to preaching, connecting with his friends and neighbors was actually Heath's favorite part of coming to church. They were all busy during the week, and he liked the way they still managed to make time for each other. Considering the good vibes that existed inside those four sturdy walls, he was pretty certain God liked it, too.

Even Tess, who normally bulldozed her way from one task to the next, slowed down enough to chat with several people as he followed her to the exit. When she paused near Paige, though, Heath braced himself for some humiliation. And he wasn't disappointed.

"So, there he is," Paige commented in a snippy tone. "The man who doesn't know how to use a phone."

"I said I was sorry," he reminded her. "Repeatedly, if I recall."

"This one," she explained to Tess, "emailed me from Alaska last year to say he was coming back for homecoming weekend and asked me to go to the football game with him. He never showed, so I sat there by myself all night. And I hate football," she added with a shudder.

Heath chuckled at the melodramatic gesture. "By yourself? I doubt that."

"Well, maybe not, but you stood me up, and I won't ever forget it."

"Obviously," he responded with a grin. "How're things other than that?"

"Same old, same old. You know how it is."

"I hear you're shaking up the town council race. Good for you."

"Oh, you," she said, playfully shoving him in the chest. "I never could stay mad at you. Take it from me, Tess. This one's as aggravating as they come, but he's still one of the best guys on the planet."

Their West Coast visitor gave him a brief once-over, ending with a coy smile. "I have no trouble believing that."

All this feminine approval was making him antsy, and out of sheer desperation, Heath focused on the other man hovering near the edge of their conversation. Offering his hand, he said, "Heath Weatherby. I'm hoping you'll save me here."

"Tyler Green. I'm in town for a few days visiting my aunt and uncle on my way to Florida. Paige and I are cousins."

The clarification was clearly for Tess's benefit, and she obliged him with a bright smile. "What a small world. Paige and I are friends."

"I have no trouble believing that." The only thing smoother than his mimicking of her was the way he said it, and Heath fought the urge to roll his eyes.

"Florida's nice this time of year," Tess commented. "Are you headed down for business or a vacation?"

"I'm a freelance ad executive and graphic designer. For the next couple of weeks, I'll be working on a media-based promotional campaign for the Miami Dolphins. The previous company made a real mess of their latest campaign, and I'll be mopping up and seeing what we can do to salvage something for this season."

"No kidding." Realizing that sounded lame, Heath tried to come up with something slightly more intelligent to follow it up. "That sounds like a big job."

"It is, but I like a challenge," Tyler responded confidently, adding a sidelong grin for Tess.

When she returned the gesture, Heath detected her more-than-casual interest in the Donaldsons' guest. In his flawless suit and tie, Tyler's polished look made Heath's own outfit seem dull by comparison. Not that it mattered to him, he reminded himself sternly. He was perfectly content with his job and the durable clothes that came with it. Of course, Tess had never eyed him with the kind of awareness she was showing Tyler.

You had to expect that when you told a

woman you just wanted to be friends, Heath supposed. That didn't mean he had to like it.

Thankfully, he and Tess were headed to the Barrett family's weekly Sunday lunch so he didn't have to examine his reaction to Tyler too closely. After saying their good-byes, they filed outside with the rest of the congregation and strolled down the sidewalk that led to Paul and Chelsea's home on Ingram Street.

"Tyler seems nice," Heath began in a conversational tone.

"Right," she commented with a quick laugh. "Seeing you guys dance around each other was like watching two boxers in the ring, sizing up their competition."

"What? I thought we were polite enough."

"For ten rounds. And while we're on the subject, what's the deal with you and Paige?"

For the life of him, he couldn't imagine why she cared. "We grew up together. Why?"

"Just curious. What made you think of going to homecoming with her?"

Her casual tone sounded forced to him, but he was at a loss for what might be driving this awkward discussion. "'Cause we're friends and she wouldn't assume it meant something if I asked her. You wouldn't believe how often that happens to me around here."

"Oh, I'd believe it," Tess corrected him with

a knowing smirk. "But I thought you were set on staying here."

"I am."

"Since you're not planning to move away, how do you expect to have that cozy little family of yours unless you settle down with someone from Barrett's Mill?"

After considering that for a moment, he sighed. "Got me there. I guess I've always figured I'll know the right woman when I see her."

"And so far you haven't?"

Any other day, he'd have easily answered that question with a no. But today, for some reason, he hesitated. Was it the blunt way she'd asked him? he wondered. Or was it something else altogether?

He wasn't one to lie, but he didn't want to give her the wrong idea, either. Shaking off his uncertainty, he said, "I guess I'm still looking."

"Yeah. Me, too." Laughter reached them from the playground in the square, and she glanced over, a wistful expression clouding her features. "Actually, I'm looking for a lot of things right now. I just wish I knew where to start finding them."

He knew that feeling all too well, and he hunted for a way to encourage her without making her feel like he'd been spying on her. "What'd you think of our little country church?"

"It's nice." Glancing back at him, she added, "I thought it would be just listening to someone talk. I really liked how everyone seemed so happy to see each other. You know, like a family."

In those simple words, he heard much more than what she'd said out loud. Like him, this uprooted city girl was searching for a place to belong. At least for him, that had meant coming home. For her, it meant starting over fresh somewhere other than where she'd grown up. Whether that was Barrett's Mill remained to be seen, but no matter what, it had to be scary for her. "I get what you mean. Knowing I could come back here after my accident made all the difference for me."

"Do you want to know what I decided during church today?"

"Sure."

Stopping in the middle of the sidewalk, she faced him squarely, determination glowing in her eyes. "I'm not going back to California at the end of the year. I'll ask if I can stay on at the mill, but if that doesn't work, I'll figure out something else. Exhausting and challenging as this week's been, it's also been the most fun I've ever had at a job. I feel like what I'm doing matters, and people pay attention to what I have to say. I totally get why Chelsea left her father's bank to work there."

"Well, she *was* in love with the owner," Heath reminded her with a grin. "I think that had something to do with her decision."

When Tess opened her mouth, the hard look on her face warned him she was about to pelt him for not taking her seriously. Then, for some reason, she stopped and gazed up at him with a thoughtful expression. He couldn't begin to imagine what she might be thinking, and he cautioned himself to be light on his feet to avoid irking her any further.

"Heath, have you ever done anything crazy for love?"

Completely unprepared for such a probing—and personal—question, he stared back at her while his mind raced to come up with a response. To his surprise, he heard himself say, "Not so far."

"Me neither. Everything I've ever done made perfect sense, at least at the time. I think that's kind of sad, don't you?"

There was a troublemaker question if ever he'd heard one. Seeking to avoid hurting her feelings, he hedged. "That depends."

"On what?"

"On whether you're happy with the results."

She gave him a give-me-a-break look, and he sighed. "Okay, I see your point. The question is, what should we do about it? I mean, individually," he added to be absolutely clear. He didn't want to muddy the friendship waters with any misunderstandings.

"I'm not sure, but things won't change if we just stand around waiting for something amazing to happen. We have to make them change."

That sounded familiar, and he grinned. "Sounds like Pastor Griggs's words of wisdom got through to you."

"Loud and clear," she agreed as they resumed their stroll. "Are all his sermons like that?"

"More or less. He and his wife have four kids and a passel of grandchildren, so he's pretty much seen it all."

"I usually hate it when people give me advice, but for some reason with him I didn't mind. I suppose it's all in the delivery. When you know someone's honestly trying to help you, with no ulterior motive, even if you don't like what they have to say, it goes down better."

Heath smothered a grin. Every day she spent in town, she sounded more like a native. It was no wonder she'd felt like there wasn't a place for her among the ambitious people she'd known in California. She had a lot more

Southern girl in her than she probably wanted to admit.

"The man's got a knack for nudging people in the right direction, that's for sure."

They spent the rest of their short walk chatting about the mill and what remained to be done before his stint as their maintenance foreman could be called a success. The subject of Tyler Green never came up, and Heath was grateful for that. Friendly by nature, his bizarre reaction to the guy bothered him, and he'd rather not examine it too closely.

In his experience, when you did that, you usually found out something about yourself you'd rather not know.

## Chapter Eight

It was a rare warm evening in late October, and Tess was enjoying some quiet time on Gram's front porch, reading the latest book from her favorite mystery author. After working at the noisy, dusty mill, the fresh air was a welcome end to her day. Pausing between chapters, she reached over to the wicker table beside her and picked up her dripping glass of sweet tea. While she drank, the call of a nightingale prompted her to glance around to find the source. She saw the bird in a nearby tree and leaned her head back to listen to its repertoire for a few lazy minutes.

Thoroughly distracted from her book, she let her gaze wander around the cozy neighborhood populated by old homes and stately trees. Every front porch was occupied by people either talking or reading actual newspapers.

The elderly couple next door was listening to a baseball game on the radio, and she marveled at how the residents of this little town enjoyed the simple things in life.

She heard the crunch of feet in the side yard and looked back over her shoulder to find Heath strolling toward her. Laughing, she teased, "I hate to be the one to tell you this, but your sneaking skills could use some work."

"Tell me about it." He grinned back, kicking a pile of dried-up leaves out of his way. "Doesn't anyone in your family own a rake?"

She loved the way he referred to the Barretts as *your family.* Knowing he viewed her as one of them cemented her growing feeling that she'd finally found her place in the world. "Uncle Tom's been here a couple times, but he can't rake them as fast as they fall. I offered to help out, but he told me it's man's work."

"That must've gone over well."

"A month ago I probably would have given him a piece of my mind."

Heath came up the porch steps and settled into the chair beside hers. He was holding a folder in his hands, and she wondered what was going on.

"And now?"

"I'm getting used to the Southern gentleman

thing," she admitted with a smile. "It kind of grows on you after a while."

"That's good, 'cause we're not planning on changing our ways just to suit you."

As much as she enjoyed sparring with him, her curiosity got the better of her. "You didn't come here just to chat, did you?"

"Well—" He drew the word out on a long drawl then shook his head. "I could use your help with something. It's important," he added emphatically, as if he feared she'd turn him down if he didn't give her a good reason to say yes.

"You don't have to talk me into it, Heath. For everything you've done to help me, I'm happy to do something to pay you back."

She held out her hand, but he pulled the folder into his chest in a protective motion that was baffling and touching at the same time. She'd never seen him act this way, and his reluctance to give up whatever was in that folder made her smile. "Please?"

"I should explain first, or it won't make sense to you."

"Okay," she agreed, curling her feet up under her and leaning on the arm of her chair. "Shoot."

He stared at her for a few anxious seconds

then took in a deep breath and began. "You know I restore cars as a side job, right?"

"I saw the old Packard you did for Bruce Harkness. He had it parked out front of The Whistlestop the other day, and he spent half an hour telling me about all the work you did on it in the last six months. It's gorgeous."

That got her a grateful smile. "Thanks. The work I do for Fred pays the bills, but I really love hauling in an old wreck no one wants and making it into what it used to be."

"Like the boys did with the mill."

"Exactly." Warming to his subject, he set the folder on the wicker table between them and faced her more squarely. "Anyway, there's a house for sale just outside of town, not far from Scott and Jenna's place. It's a Cape with a nice yard, but what I'm really after is the original carriage barn out back. If I expanded it, it'd make a great workshop."

"I remember you saying you had a lead on your own place. Is this the one?"

"Yeah." Giving her a sheepish grin, he said, "I gotta admit, I'm kinda surprised you remember that. When I talk about it, most folks pretend they're listening, but next time I see them, they can't seem to recall any of it."

"I'm not like that," she reminded him, adding an encouraging smile. "I'm guessing there's more you want to tell me. Go ahead."

While he outlined his ideas for her, his eyes shone with excitement. He made her think of a little boy talking about the cool tree house he was going to build, and she hid a smile to avoid making him think she wasn't taking him seriously. When he finished she tapped the folder. "Are these the plans?"

"Yeah. The problem is, I need a zoning variance to run a business in that spot. Bruce invited me to make a pitch at this week's town meeting, but I've never done anything like that so I'm not quite sure how to go about it."

"And you're asking me for my input?" When he nodded, she was equal parts flattered and confused. "Why?"

"You're smart, and you have good judgment and business sense."

"Scott's like that, too. Besides which, you guys have been best friends forever. Why me?"

He hesitated for a moment then gave her one of those irresistible grins. "Okay, you got me. I picked you 'cause you're way nicer to look at."

If the artless compliment had come from anyone else, she'd have bristled and scolded him for being a chauvinistic caveman. Since it was Heath, she took it in stride and opened the folder. Inside were honest-to-goodness blueprints, with the stamp of an architecture firm that listed an address in downtown Roanoke.

"You really went all-out for this," she said while she flipped through the different site views. "How big is the property?"

"Two acres. I'll leave half the land for the house and use the rest for the shop. Should be plenty since I'll only be working on one car at a time."

"What if your business takes off? You might need a storage building for cars waiting to be restored."

"That's this right here." He pointed to a sketched-in square with dimensions but no detail. Moving his finger along, he continued. "This will be the painting shed, and this is a paved lot with room for ten cars. Twelve if you park 'em right."

"What are you going to call it?"

That one stopped him in his tracks. "I haven't thought about that."

"Every business needs a name," she pointed out as gently as she could. "If nothing else, you need to print something on your business cards."

"I've been so focused on the building part of it, I haven't had a chance to consider all that." Leaning back, he crossed a boot over his knee with a frown. "Any ideas?"

Tess was struck by how readily he asked her for her opinion, as if he actually valued her input. That happened at the mill often enough these days, she'd gotten used to it. But coming from this fiercely independent man, it was another thing altogether. Humbled by his faith in her, she took her time coming up with a response.

Seeking inspiration, she mentally strolled through the area so many generations of local families had called home. The town with its quaint buildings and pretty central green, the miles of forest that led from there out to the mill that had produced the lumber used to build all these sturdy homes and businesses that had stood the test of time.

And in the distance, the Blue Ridge Mountains loomed over it all, rugged and beautiful from their uppermost peaks to the shadows of the lowest valley. Smiling at the vision in her head, she turned back to Heath. "How about Blue Ridge Classics?"

"Wow." His stunned look spread into a broad grin. "That's perfect. How'd you come up with it off the top of your head like that?"

"I'm not sure," she admitted with a shrug. "It just popped in."

"I think you missed your calling. With that

kind of imagination, you should be a writer or something."

He was closer to the truth than he knew, and she debated whether to continue their conversation or change the subject. Since he'd laid out his dreams for her, she decided there was no harm in doing the same herself. "I love to read, but I'm not much for creative writing. I've always been interested in advertising, though. I took some marketing classes in college, and I thought the whole industry was fascinating."

"Why didn't you go into that?"

"Too much work," she confided with a sigh. "I just wanted the degree to keep my parents happy, so I went with psychology."

"Knowing why people act the way they do is part of advertising, right?"

"I guess."

"So you were just getting started," he suggested in a helpful tone. "If you want to get serious about it, you can go back to school and take those classes you're missing. When you're done, you can use all those smarts you've got and make a nice career for yourself."

"Do you have any idea how competitive that industry is? In LA, you can't swing a cat without hitting an ad executive who's hunting for a job." For some reason, he grinned, and she demanded, "Did I say something funny?"

The grin widened, and he said, "*Swing a cat.* Hate to break this to you, magpie, but you're turning into one of us country folk."

"Wonderful," she grumbled with a mock frown. She couldn't keep it up in the face of his amusement, though, and she relented with a sigh. "Whatever. There's worse things to be, I suppose."

"I won't argue with that."

The twinkle was back in his eyes, but it had a different quality to it this time. Warmer, deeper, as if he meant that look to be especially for her. It was unsettling, and she did her best to break that intimate connection with him.

The trouble was, she couldn't make herself look away. Desperate to regain her composure, she recalled the folder sitting on the table between them. Forcing herself to look at it instead of him, she said, "So, your pitch. I'm assuming since Bruce is the mayor, he'll be running the meeting."

"Right."

Heath didn't move, but his gaze was as intense as ever, and she sternly cautioned herself to stick with the project. She had a strong feeling that if she mentioned anything even remotely personal, things between them could slide out of her control in a heartbeat.

To her dismay, the thought of getting closer

to Heath didn't terrify her anymore. In fact, if he gave her the slightest hint that he was beginning to view her as more than a friend, she wasn't sure she had the resolve to push him back into the nice, safe box she'd been keeping him in.

"Then I think your best opening is to bring up that beautiful Packard of his," she suggested in her most professional tone. "People know how good you are with modern cars, but they might not realize you take on other projects, too. Everyone's seen his car around town, and that will prove how serious you are about your business."

"Great idea." Jotting down a note, he refocused on her with genuine interest. "Then what?"

While she outlined a strategy for him to use, she was surprised at how easily the concepts and their execution came to her. The more they talked, the more she was leaning toward taking his advice about taking more classes. She could start out at the local community college to make sure she was headed in the right direction, and then sign up for some online courses offered by a larger school.

The irony of it was that her father would heartily approve of her going into advertising, but not for the reasons that made it so appealing to her. He'd value the money-making potential in that industry, not the creative aspects of it that she was so drawn to.

Because sadly, nothing in her old life had changed. The best thing she could do was leave it behind and move on.

"While I'm here," Heath broke in, "I was wondering if you still need some help with your scarecrow?"

"All I can get. Jason came by with his truck earlier, dropped off three bales of straw and saluted on his way out. According to him," she added in a sour tone, "Chelsea handled the whole thing on her own last year, and the boys aren't exactly the artsy-craftsy types."

Her guest laughed then abruptly stopped when she didn't join in. His puzzled look gave way to understanding, and he said, "Insulting, huh?"

"I'd take it to heart if I didn't know how busy he and Scott are, trying to take up some of the load for Paul so he can be home more. I thought about asking Chelsea for help with the design, but I'd hate for her to find out I put it off this long. It might stress her out more than she already is."

His brow furrowed with genuine concern. "She and the baby are doing okay, though, right?"

"Some days are better than others."

It wasn't like her to be so open about problems, and the worry she heard in her voice made her cringe. Reaching over, Heath rested a comforting hand over hers. "We're all praying for them, Tess. Every day that goes by, the baby's a little bit stronger."

"I know." She began to well up and did her best to blink away the tears. "I just hope it's enough."

"You're doing what you can to make things easier for Chelsea. Now you need to have a little faith."

"I'm not good at that. Yet," she added quickly, brushing at a tear that had broken free and was edging down her cheek. "I'm getting better, though."

"Yeah, you are." Giving her an encouraging smile, he got to his feet and held out his hand. "Meantime, a good distraction will help get your mind onto something else. What say we go build us a scarecrow?"

Realizing his suggestion was much better than fretting over something she had no control over, she gulped down her fear and stood up. His hand was within reach, and she debated the wisdom of accepting his kind gesture. While she was still hesitant to encourage him that way, part of her longed to tap into the strength that seemed to be built into this kind-hearted man.

In the end, logic gave way to emotion, and she took his hand. "Okay. Where should we start?"

"Well, some folks do a single scarecrow, and others put together a scene. Which do you like better?"

"Which kind usually wins?"

Chuckling, he slid open the door to Gram's garage and snapped on the light inside. "Spoken like a true Barrett. The scenes win most years 'cause they're about something folks can relate to."

"Like what?"

"Farmers, carpenters, mechanics, stuff like that."

His list got her wheels spinning, and an idea popped up that was so crazy, she was tempted to reject it immediately. But the longer she considered it, the more it seemed completely appropriate for this year's Harvest Festival.

Up on a shelf, she noticed a box labeled "Will's treasures" and pulled it down to see what was inside. Taking out a faded Atlanta Braves cap and a folded-up fishing rod, she showed them to Heath. "What do you think?"

"I'm not sure. What're you getting at?"

"This is the family's first Thanksgiving

without Granddad. Do you think they'd like it if we did something to honor him?"

"You mean, dress up a scarecrow like Will?" When she nodded, Heath rewarded her with a bright grin. "They'd love it. He'd get a kick out of it, too."

He said that with such conviction, she felt stupid for not following along. After pondering it for several seconds, she shook her head in frustration. "You're not making any sense. He's not here to see it, so how could he like it?"

"Folks pass on all the time." Grabbing a bale of straw in each hand, he tossed them through the door and into the driveway as if they didn't weigh a thing. "But if we keep their memory alive, they're never really gone."

"Sorry?"

"You can't think it through, Tess." He chided her like a parent correcting a child. "You have to feel it."

A glimmer of understanding started deep inside her, growing brighter as she gradually caught on. "You mean, like how I feel closer to him when I'm at the mill? Or driving that old truck?"

"Exactly. Will loved those things, and there's a big part of him left in them. The fact that you feel so attached to them is how you know you're a Barrett."

"I've always been a Barrett," she protested, confused all over again.

Heath gave her a long look then slowly shook his head. "That's been your name all this time, but you didn't know much about your history. Now you do, and you recognize how special it is. *That's* what makes you part of the family that founded this town."

"And my dad isn't," she commented pensively. "He never wanted to be."

"I'm not sure why, but yeah, that's how I see it. Did you ever ask him why he left?"

She shook her head. "All he ever told us was he was from a backwater town in Virginia. He made it sound like a hole in the ground or something. Anyway, Jenna and I met when she was in California for an art show a couple years ago. If that hadn't happened, I probably wouldn't have gotten an invitation to their wedding."

"Interesting." A grin slowly worked its way across his rugged features, ending in a bright expression that warmed her down to her toes. "Makes you wonder if God had something in mind, doesn't it?"

"For us, you mean?" Much as she'd disparaged her grandmother's determined attempt at matchmaking, Tess's poor opinion of it had gradually changed over the last couple of weeks. These days the notion of being linked with Heath wasn't nearly as panic-inducing as it once was.

"Sure, why not?" Taking the folding knife from its sheath on his belt, he sliced through the twine holding the bales together. "You can never have too many friends, right?"

"Right," she replied automatically as her foolish heart thudded into the gravel at her feet.

It figured, she moped silently while she helped him separate the bales into more manageable sections of straw. Just when she thought she might be ready to explore something more serious with someone, he wasn't interested.

If that happy family of her dreams was ever going to be a reality, she really needed to work on her timing.

"What'd you do to this monster, anyway?" Heath grumbled while he and Scott were laboring to get the enormous dust vac in Scott's woodworking shop functioning again.

"Nothing to warrant it blowing up on me like this," he insisted in a wounded tone. "I clean it every other day so it doesn't get clogged, and the filter's still a mess."

"It is forty years old. Might have something to do with it."

"Well, I need you to do your thing 'cause I'm not gonna have money for a new one for a long time."

Something in his voice got Heath's attention, and he stared over at his childhood friend for a few seconds before it clicked. "Jenna's pregnant, isn't she?"

"What?" he choked, his eyes just about bugging out of his head. "Get a grip, man. We just got married."

Despite the scolding, Heath sensed he was on the right track. "But you're thinking about it?"

"She is. I'm still not sure, but it's tough to keep saying no to her. We just want to save up as much money as we can so we're ready for whatever happens."

"In case she has the same problems Chelsea is."

"Yeah," Scott admitted on a heavy sigh. "I got no idea how Paul handles everything day in and day out. When stuff breaks, guys like you and me just fix it, y'know?"

"But you can't do that with people. I get it." His hand was covered in grime, but he knew Scott wouldn't care, so they traded one of those solid handshakes guys used instead of words. That didn't seem like enough this time, so Heath added, "You need anything, let me know."

"Thanks." The moment passed quickly, and his old buddy returned to the task at hand. "Right now I need you to fix this vac so I can finish sanding this cabinet and get it stained."

He punctuated his comment with a swift kick to the metal housing, and Heath chuckled. "That doesn't work any better now than when we were six."

Delving deeper into the outdated mechanism, he located a cracked part that was dangling free rather than doing its job. Before removing it, he took his phone from his pocket and snapped photos from several different angles so he'd know how to replace it later on. Then he twisted it loose and put it on a nearby workbench.

He was hunting for more problems when Scott asked, "So, I heard you and Tess are working on the mill's scarecrow together. How's that going?"

"Fine," he grunted as he stripped out a worn drive belt. "Why?"

"No reason. It's just you both like being in charge, and I was wondering how you're getting along."

Angling his head, Heath gave him a long,

suspicious look. "Why don't you just spit out whatever you're trying not to say?"

"Fine." Glaring at him over the back of the hutch he was sanding, Scott was suddenly sober as a judge. "Have you got designs on my cousin?"

"'Course not. We're friends is all."

Folding his arms in his customary arguing stance, Scott barked out a laugh. "Don't try that on me, Weatherby. I know just how friendly you can get."

"Tess is different," he blurted without thinking how those words would sound to someone else. It was the truth, though, and he tried to sort through his jumbled feelings about her so he could explain what he meant. "She's got a great sense of humor, and she's smart as a whip. Smarter than me, probably."

"Definitely, but go on."

"Anyway," Heath continued in a deliberate tone, "I've been wanting to ask her out, but she's used to expensive restaurants and fancy vacations. I'm more of a picnic-in-the-woods kinda guy."

"This time of year, with the views you get out there, that's a good choice."

Heath eyed him warily. After all, this was his cousin they were discussing. While the Barrett boys didn't have any sisters, Heath was confident if they had, those girls' prospective boyfriends would have been forced to run a pretty intimidating gauntlet before a date.

"Are you actually being helpful for a change?" he asked.

"Aw, come on. Here I am trying to be nice, and you're gonna give me a hard time?"

"I appreciate the effort," Heath retorted in a tone drenched with sarcasm. "I know it's a stretch for you."

Scott heaved a long-suffering sigh. "Tell me about it. I think Jenna's finally wearing me down."

They traded a male look then broke up laughing. When they finally quieted down, Heath said, "Okay, so I've got your blessing on this, but Tess is another story. You have any ideas for me?"

"She thinks you're some kind of hero for helping out at the mill, so you've already got points on the board. Then there's the truck and the scarecrow." He ticked them off on his fingers before going on. "For some strange reason, she likes you the way you are. My advice is just be yourself and hope for the best."

"Great," Heath mumbled, shaking his head. "Thanks a lot."

"Hey, it worked for me."

True enough, Heath acknowledged as he

got back to work on the broken vacuum. Now that he thought about it, on paper none of the Barrett boys should be with the women they'd married. Somehow, they'd all connected with women generous and patient enough to love them despite their many obvious shortcomings.

If his friends could find a way to make that happen, maybe he could, too.

## Chapter Nine

"Hey there." Paige stood and greeted Tess with a bright smile when she arrived at the town meeting on Thursday night. "When I mentioned this to you, I never thought you'd actually come."

"You made it sound like so much fun, I couldn't stay away."

Her new friend moved down a spot then seemed to notice something over Tess's shoulder and moved down one more. "Hey, Heath. You never come to these things. What're you doing here?"

"Came to see what all the fuss is about," he replied smoothly. Tess noticed the folder he was carrying and marveled at how cool he sounded despite the very important business he planned to bring up this evening.

"Really? I don't remember you ever showing the slightest interest in what's going on around here."

"Well, I'm here tonight. What's up with you these days, squirt?"

Paige groaned. "Please don't call me that. I'm all grown up, and it's bad enough to hear it from my brothers."

These two were like a comedy team, and now that she had some experience with her mischievous cousins, Tess appreciated the good-natured teasing more than she'd have thought possible only a month ago. Laughing, she asked, "How many brothers do you have?"

"Four, all older. Imagine if you'd grown up here, with the Barrett boys hovering over your shoulder, scaring off every guy in town." Paige heaved a melodramatic sigh. "It's awful."

"Did you ever think of moving away?" Tess asked as the three of them sat down.

"No," Paige answered immediately. "Living in Barrett's Mill might not be ideal for me, but it's home."

"Amen to that," Heath agreed heartily, adding a fist bump for good measure.

Not for the first time, Tess wished she could feel that way about where she'd grown up. Unfortunately, she'd never felt completely at ease in the gated community with a pool in every yard and luxury cars in every garage.

This town, with its historical vibe and firmly grounded residents, was proving to be much more her style.

"Nice outfit," Heath said, as if he'd sensed her meandering thoughts. "Is it new?"

During their shopping trip, Paige had talked her into buying the faded jeans and girly flannel shirt, and her fashion adviser grinned triumphantly. "See? I told you. Where's the jacket?"

"Hanging on a hook in the entryway. Why?"

"It's even cuter with the jacket," Paige replied, as if the answer should have been obvious.

When she turned away to talk with an elderly man seated behind them, Heath leaned in to murmur, "Y'know, she's usually right about that kinda stuff. She picked out my tux for prom, and I looked fantastic."

"Oh, you probably look good in anything."

The compliment slipped out before she realized what she was saying, and she clamped her mouth shut to keep any more incriminating statements under wraps. Heath had been a good friend and champion for her since their odd encounter on her first morning at the mill. She didn't want to risk losing that because a small—very small—part of her wondered how it would feel to take the ultimate leap into a relationship with him.

Thankfully, he didn't say anything, just gave her an aw-shucks grin that made her want to smile back. "Thanks."

"Like you've never heard that before." With his muscular build and surfer-dude looks, the talented mechanic was by far the best-looking guy she'd ever met. When you added in his warm, friendly manner, the guy was one step short of irresistible. She really had to stop, she scolded herself. If she didn't, she'd start saying these things out loud, and then where would she be?

He locked gazes with her, and the color of his eyes warmed to a deep cobalt. "Not from you."

Dazed by his uncharacteristic intensity, Tess sat there with her mouth open, desperately hunting for a pithy comeback. Convinced he was ribbing her, she searched his expression for that humorous twinkle she often found there.

This time, though, he appeared to be totally serious. It struck her as odd coming from the guy who kept insisting they were just friends, and fortunately, the mayor saved her by calling the meeting to order.

After reading the minutes from their previous session, he moved on to current business, which centered around next week's Harvest Festival. It seemed like everyone was involved in one way or another, and she had to admit they were much more organized than she'd anticipated.

Once they'd finished going over details for the festival, the mayor asked if anyone wanted to bring up any new business. Heath traded a hesitant look with her then raised his hand, waiting for a nod to continue.

Standing, he squared those broad shoulders of his and began. "I've got my eye on the Cape out on the edge of town that's recently gone up for sale."

Tucking his hands into the front pockets of his jeans, he appeared calm and under control. But because she was sitting next to him, Tess caught the slight curl of his fingers that betrayed the fact that under all that mellow, he was nervous. She knew what a significant step this new venture would be for him, and she listened carefully, willing him to make his case the way they'd discussed.

Glancing around the crowd, he went on. "For any of you who don't know, I've been doing car restorations on the side for the last few months. Fred's been nice enough to let me use his bay space when I need it." He added a smile for his boss. "But I'd like to be able to work on things at home, too. So I'm asking for a zoning variance to allow that kind of business in the neighborhood. I'd be changing the property quite a bit, adding a parking lot and expanding the garage to accommodate three bays and a workshop."

Hearing him outline his plans and answer questions from the group, Tess was impressed by his pragmatic approach and businesslike tone. While she knew firsthand what a talented mechanic he was, this was a side of him she'd never have imagined in a million years. Sure, she'd given him some advice on how to structure his pitch, but he was the one who had to convince the town to bend the rules for him. Sneaking a glance around the group, she noticed several nods in support of his proposal.

Apparently, there was a lot more to this easygoing country boy than met the eye, she thought with a little grin. Interesting.

Once Heath finished his presentation, the mayor asked, "Are there any more questions?" No one responded, and he gave Heath a thoughtful look. "Since it's you, I'm inclined to rubber-stamp this, but we have to go through channels the same way we would for anyone else. Submit your building plans to the town council, and we'll take a look at what you've got in mind. Fair enough?"

"Yes, sir. Thank you." Sending a look around the room, he grinned like a little boy who'd just discovered his dream puppy was on its way. "All of you."

Everyone broke into applause, and he acknowledged it with a raised hand before sitting back down. Even though she knew people were watching, Tess reached over and squeezed his hand. "Nice job."

"Thanks," he breathed with understandable relief. "That was slightly terrifying."

"You did great," she assured him, nudging his shoulder with hers. "And if anyone gives you a hard time, you let me know. I'll march down to that council meeting and set them straight."

He met her offer with a chuckle. "I've got the Barrett bulldog on my side. Good to know."

"The Barrett bulldog," she echoed quietly. Only a few weeks ago, she'd have found the moniker insulting. But now that she understood where he was coming from, she took it for the compliment he meant it to be. "I like it."

"I thought you might. Speaking of which, Bruce and Molly keep The Whistlestop open late on town meeting nights. Most folks head over there afterward, and I'd imagine Molly's cooked up some things you'd like."

Raising an eyebrow, Tess gave him a curious look. "Are you asking me out?"

"That depends," he joked with another one of his playful grins. "What's your answer?"

Was this his way of telling her she wasn't the only one feeling more than camaraderie between them lately? She figured there was only one way to find out. "Sure, why not? When in Rome, right?"

"Right."

Despite the fact that he'd agreed with her, the long look he gave her made her wonder if being so flip about his invitation had been a mistake. There was no fixing it now, so she shrugged it off and tuned back in to the meeting. Next on the agenda was the thorny problem of how to keep a local farmer's wandering roosters out of his neighbor's chicken coop. Apparently, the males were the wrong sort of chickens to be mixing with the hens, and it was becoming quite the problem. Before long, the discussion grew heated, and Tess found herself wishing she had some popcorn.

"Are these meetings always like this?" she whispered to Heath.

"I'm not here much, but from what I hear they all go this way. Bruce never lets things get outta hand, though, and everyone ends up at the diner for pie."

What a great way to handle problems, she thought with a grin. If more folks could settle their disagreements over dessert, the world would be a happier place.

The wandering poultry issue was settled with a reasonable compromise for both farmers to install extra fences to keep the animals from causing any more trouble. While Bruce closed the meeting, Tess wasn't sure why the farmers couldn't have come to that conclusion on their own. She said as much while she and Heath filed out with the others, and he laughed.

"Mostly, folks want to have their time in the spotlight, I guess. If they get a ruling in their favor, it's gravy."

"So the people who bring up issues at these meetings don't really care who's right or wrong? That's nuts."

"That's Barrett's Mill," he said with a grin. "Gotta love it."

They crossed the street to where The Whistlestop was fully lit up and ready for business. People rapidly filled the booths and tables, and she heard snippets of conversation about tonight's gathering, tomorrow's forecast and whether or not Washington's injured running back would be ready for Sunday's football game.

Simple things, she mused while she sipped her water. Nothing earth-shattering, but they were woven into the fabric of existence here. Timeless and comforting, because from week to week and year to year, they didn't change all that much. The world might be on a crazy spiral, but this Blue Ridge town stayed on its even keel by focusing on what mattered most: Family, friends and faith.

When you had those, she realized with stunning certainty, everything else in your life fell into its proper place. And when you were missing them, nothing ever felt quite right. So all these years that she'd been trying to find a way to be happy, she'd been looking in the wrong place.

True contentment came from inside a person. You could dress your life up in the most extravagant style you could afford, but it wouldn't make a bit of difference if you didn't have people to love, who loved you back. And without faith, no matter how hard you tried, none of what you wished for would ever come to be.

Stunned by her epiphany, she looked across the table at Heath, who was turned around in his seat, chatting with Fred Morgan about something too mechanical for her to follow. Had God brought her here? More than that, had He intended all along for her to end up in the one place where she'd find a man who could accept and appreciate her the way she was?

She couldn't deny that Heath had patiently and often firmly encouraged her to accept the bad things in her past while looking toward the future. His own trials had given her an example to follow, and his upbeat approach to life made it easier for her to be hopeful about the changes she was making in her own.

When he turned back around, she gathered up her courage and said, "Heath?"

"Yeah?"

Those impossibly blue eyes focused on her with a warmth she could no longer deny. But this time instead of ignoring it, she let herself return the look. "I want to thank you for everything you've done to help me since I got here. No one's ever tried so hard with me, and I really appreciate it."

"It wasn't easy," he acknowledged with a low chuckle, "but I figured you were worth it."

"I can't imagine why."

"Not everything has an explanation, Tess. Sometimes we just have to believe."

Reaching out, he covered one of her hands with his much larger one. She felt his strength pulsing just below the surface, and the sensation comforted her in a way she'd never experienced with anyone before. For someone who'd promised herself she'd find a way to be more independent, the thought of relying on this wonderful man was both tempting and terrifying.

Doing her best to remain composed in the middle of the restaurant, she said, "Someday that might actually make sense to me."

"It will. I just hope I'm there to see it."

Smiling, she angled her fingers to give his hand a little squeeze. "Me, too."

Their waitress chose that precise moment to stop for their orders, and Tess fully expected Heath to pull back and retreat to his side of the table. He didn't. Instead, he twined his fingers through hers in a blatant display of something more than friendship.

Disappointment dimmed the young woman's eyes as she jotted down their dessert order. As she headed for the kitchen, she cast a wistful look back over her shoulder at Heath, and Tess murmured, "I think she has a crush on you."

"Well, now, that's a shame." He gave her the grin that had charmed her the very first time they met. "'Cause I've got a crush on you."

"You do not."

"Yeah, I do." He let out a heavy sigh. "I'm not sure why, but I do."

Hearing those words come out of his mouth made her heart do a little flip.

*Tell him, Tess*, a little voice whispered in her head. *Tell him how you feel*.

The last time she did that, it ended in disaster. But this was now, and Heath was so unlike Avery, they might have been two entirely different species. So she swallowed her fear and took the biggest, bravest leap of her life. "Actually, I know what you mean, because I feel the same way about you."

His eyes met hers in a hopeful look that confirmed she'd made the right decision. A delighted little boy's grin worked its way across his face, and he said, "That's good to know."

That didn't even come close to expressing the emotions churning through her right now, and she laughed. "Heath Weatherby, ladies and gentlemen. Master of understatement."

"You have the greatest laugh. Seems like you do it a lot more now than when you first got here."

"I have more reason to these days. I really like it here."

"Yeah? What do you like best?"

"The people," she told him with a fond smile. "They're the best."

Their lovelorn waitress returned with their desserts and the check, which she plunked down in front of Tess. With a dismissive flounce of her shoulder, she pivoted away to greet her next customer in a syrupy voice that left no doubt about her opinion of Tess.

"Something tells me we're not going to be best friends anytime soon," she muttered as she dug into a lemon meringue pie that stood several inches high.

"Don't let her get to you, darlin'. You've always got me."

If that smooth Southern line had come out of anyone else's mouth, she'd have cut him off at the knees. But since it was Heath, she laughed it off. "Is that a good thing or a bad thing?"

"Dunno," he replied around a mouthful of pecan pie. Swallowing, he winked at her. "I guess we'll have fun finding out."

# Chapter Ten

"How's this?"

Grinning like a little kid at the fair, Tess plucked the fishing pole from Scarecrow Will's hand and slung it over her shoulder like a pro. The annual Harvest Festival was in full swing, and the town square was crammed with people from all over the area. Heath could hear the clang of the Strong Man game and the sound of scattering pins as a guy in a letterman jacket threw a strike to win his cheerleader girlfriend a life-size stuffed unicorn.

Over it all wafted the scents of fresh popcorn drenched in butter, and sugar and cinnamon from stands selling fried dough and Helen Morgan's prize-winning pralines. The weather had cooperated, and the clear sky was dotted with stars that brought to mind the display of diamond rings on black velvet he'd once seen in a jewelry store. He didn't know why he was thinking of that now, but when Tess did a model's turn and laughed, the reason was as clear to him as anything had ever been.

Not that he was planning to propose anytime soon, of course. But spending a fun evening with a beautiful woman tended to make a guy start considering the possibilities.

Chuckling, he lined up the shot in the viewfinder of his camera phone. "If I didn't know better, I might think you were one of those tomboys who baits her own hook."

"Ewww!"

She scrunched up her nose just as he snapped the picture, and he saved it because he knew every time he looked at it, he'd bust out laughing. "Sorry, bad shot. Let's get one more."

This one was better, and just in time, too. From out of nowhere, several Barretts crowded around, eager for a look at this year's contest entry. Tess had kept her idea secret from everyone but Heath, and he stepped back to let everyone get a closer view.

"Granddad would love it," Jason announced confidently, patting the straw man's baseball cap.

"He'd have laughed himself silly," Olivia agreed with a fond smile. When she reached out to straighten the collar on the flannel shirt, the touching gesture made Heath stop and think. She and Will had been married for more than sixty years, and while he knew there had been some tough times, they'd faced them together. Even in his final days, Olivia had stayed by Will's side, tirelessly caring for him, making sure he was as comfortable as she could make him.

Heath wanted that kind of love. The kind that took a beating and still stood tall, the way his parents' had. That was why he was still single, he recognized soberly. Judging by the number of divorces among his friends, not every couple could make that till-death-do-us-part promise and keep it.

But tonight was for celebrating, not brooding. Heath pushed aside the serious stuff and said, "How 'bout we get all the Barretts in there? We'll give Paige a family photo for her new town newsletter."

"Make sure you get my good side," Scott warned.

His wife angled a bemused look over her shoulder at him. "Do you have one?"

The others laughed at that, and Scott made a face at her. "Ha-ha, very funny."

"I thought so," she replied with a satisfied smirk.

"Good evening, everyone," Pastor Griggs

greeted them as he hurried past, a huge blue pin that read *Pie Judge* flapping against his chest. "Don't forget to come by and cast your votes for the scarecrows."

And with that, he was gone, spreading his message to a group of people milling around a tent sporting a sign for *Tastes of Autumn*. It smelled like every kind of pie and cake you could imagine, and Heath made a mental note to check it out later. All the proceeds went to local charities, and he had every intention of taking full advantage of all the talented Southern cooks who'd donated their best work to this year's festival.

As if she'd read his mind, Tess popped up beside him with a candied apple in one hand and a corn dog in the other. "Take your pick."

"Which one did you buy first?"

"The apple."

"Then I'll take the dog."

While he was chewing, she tilted her head at him with a curious expression. "Why did you ask me that?"

Swallowing, he answered, "I figured you bought your favorite thing first, so I left it for you."

"That's really sweet. And totally accurate," she added with a bright smile. Biting into the apple, she glanced around at the crowd. "I thought I'd pretty much met everyone by now. I had no idea there were so many people living in Barrett's Mill."

"Some of 'em are from other towns. There aren't a lot of places that do this kind of thing anymore."

"I've only seen stuff like this in movies," she commented. "It's really nice."

She had a bit of red candy on her cheek, and he almost reached out to wipe it away for her. Instead, he tapped his own face. "You've got a little right here."

"Thanks." She swiped at it with her fingertip and gave him a questioning look. When he nodded, she said, "I've been to lots of great events over the years, but I can't remember ever having a better time."

"I'm glad you're enjoying yourself. Any take on how the contest is going?"

"Paige is probably gonna win," Tess admitted without a trace of envy. "I mean, really, who could beat the *American Gothic* couple done up as Bruce and Molly Harkness?"

"American Scarecrow. It's a classic."

They both laughed, and he barely heard the ringtone on Tess's phone. When she pulled it from the pocket of her denim jacket, she abruptly went still. "It's Paul."

Suddenly, the lighthearted evening took on

an ominous chill, and he gently tugged her to a quieter spot amid the chaos. She answered the call then listened in stony silence for a few seconds.

"I'll round up everyone here and we'll meet you at the hospital. Give Chelsea a hug from me."

Her hands were shaking when she ended the call, and she gazed up at Heath with eyes that were rapidly filling with tears. "Chelsea's not doing well."

That was all he needed to hear. Wrapping his arms around her, Heath felt her leaning against him as if she couldn't stand on her own. After a few moments she regained her composure and drew back. "I have to tell everyone and get to Cambridge."

She was still trembling, and she dropped her phone into the grass. Heath picked it up and tucked it in his own pocket before texting Scott.

Baby in trouble. Hospital now.

"We walked here," Tess said in a dazed voice. "I have to go get Gram's car."

"Not a chance," he corrected her sternly. "You're in no shape to drive anywhere. I'll take you."

"You don't have to—"

"You gonna stand here arguing with me or get moving?"

The woeful look she gave him drove deep into his heart. "Heath, I'm scared. What if she loses the baby?"

"She won't," he assured her, taking her hands to steady them. "Chelsea's strong, and this is just a few weeks early. The baby might be a little small, but they've got a top-notch maternity unit in Cambridge. They'll know what to do."

He recognized he was saying that as much for his own benefit as hers, but his words eased some of the terror from her eyes. "Okay. We should get going, then."

Seeking to avoid a lot of awkward questions that would only slow them down, he put an arm around her shoulders and cut across the green to where he'd parked his truck earlier. Several other cars were already running, and he fell in line behind the procession of Barretts hurrying toward Cambridge.

*Please, God*, he prayed as he turned onto the highway. *Let everything be okay.*

When they arrived at the hospital, Uncle Tom and Aunt Diane led them to the maternity ward. Paul must have warned the staff that the family was on its way, because the large group of near-frantic people was met by a plump redheaded nurse wearing rubber ducky scrubs and a name tag that said Nancy.

The first thing she did was pull Diane into a fierce hug. Then she grasped her friend's shoulders and said, "You know we're the best around, right?"

Diane swallowed hard but somehow managed to nod. "Thanks, Nan."

"Oh, don't even." Holding out her arms, she gave the rest of them a reassuring, motherly smile. "I know you're all worried, and I've cleared a spot in the family waiting area for you. Paul and Chelsea are in with their doctor right now, and we'll get you some news the second we have it."

Her white shoes squeaked on the freshly buffed floor as she pivoted and escorted them down a hallway whose walls were painted with pink and blue clouds and decorated with pictures of happy mothers holding their infants. Motioning them into an empty alcove dotted with comfy-looking chairs, she continued through and out the far door, leaving the Barretts to settle in as much as they could. Worried looks flew from one person to another, even though Heath could see the guys were doing their best to keep everyone calm.

"It'll be fine." Jason's optimism didn't match up with the concern he was obviously feeling, but Heath gave him credit for trying. "This way, little William Henry can catch his first Thanksgiving football game now instead of having to wait for next year."

"That's the spirit," Diane approved, rubbing his shoulder. "We have to think positive."

After about half an hour of waiting and trying not to stare at the clock, Heath noticed some motion in the hallway Nurse Nan had gone down earlier. Through the narrow window in the door, he saw a familiar figure all but running toward the room where they were sitting. "There's Paul."

The father-to-be was dressed in blue scrubs, and a nurse stopped him, pointing to the floor. Clearly agitated, he stripped off the booties covering his shoes and just about blasted the door off its hinges when he flung it open.

"It's bad," Tess whispered, her face white with fear. "He looks terrified."

Heath didn't know what to say, but he took her cold hand in his and offered what he hoped was a comforting look. When Paul reached the family huddle, he held out his hands in a silencing gesture.

"This has to be quick. Chelsea's stable, but the baby's in major distress. They're keeping an eye on things, but if they don't improve, Dr. Weber's doing an emergency C-section."

Standing, Tom embraced his son and then gently pushed him away. "Go and take care of Chelsea. We'll be here praying."

"I know." Paul's brave front wavered, and he glanced around the room with a grateful smile.

Then he was gone.

Tess had been staring at the TV suspended from the ceiling, not seeing much of anything. When the local news station signed off and the national anthem came on, a waving American flag told her it was midnight. They still hadn't heard anything about the baby, and she'd lost track of Heath. She vaguely recalled him giving her a quick hug before promising to be back soon. She had no clue how long ago that was, but now she was starting to worry about him, too.

"Hey, cuz." Scott threw himself into the chair beside her and angled a look over at her. "How're you holding up?"

"Okay. How about you?"

"Same."

Obviously out of topics to discuss with her, he glanced around the large niche Nancy had reserved for them. The walls were painted a mellow peach color that was probably meant to soothe visitors' nerves, but for some reason it made Tess think of sherbet. Which reminded her that all she'd had to eat since lunch was part of a candied apple.

As if on cue from some unseen movie director, Heath backed through one of the closed double doors carrying a huge box labeled Paper Towels.

"When I told them you were all here, Molly and Bruce opened The Whistlestop kitchen and got busy," he explained as he set the carton down on a low table. "There's three more of these in my truck."

Jason and Scott jumped up to help him, and before long Diane and Olivia had set out an impromptu buffet for their hungry crew. Molly had thought of everything, from meals in divided containers to coffee carafes filled with her heady brew.

"Aw, yeah," Heath grunted his approval after gulping some down. "That's the stuff."

Famished as she'd been just a few minutes ago, now the sight of food made Tess queasy. She picked at her meal, waiting for her stomach to settle. As always, Heath noticed what she was doing, and he leaned in to murmur, "Start with the bread. It's fresh."

Grateful for the suggestion and the discreet way he delivered it, she dredged up a faint smile and buttered the roll. After a few tentative bites, her appetite returned, and she moved on to the chicken.

"Better?" he asked.

"A little, thanks."

"Anytime."

That was his usual response when she thanked him for something, and up until now, she'd assumed it was just a habit he'd developed. But now that she'd seen him in action during various crises, she realized that *anytime* meant he'd be there whenever she needed him, the way he'd been since she nearly crashed into him.

Somehow, through no talent of her own, here in the backwoods of Virginia she'd discovered a caring, dependable man who didn't shrink away from trouble but rose to meet it. Despite the problems he'd faced, he approached life with strength and humor, relying on his faith to help him absorb the twists and turns that came his way. And as if that wasn't enough, through his calm, steady example, he'd taught her how to do the same.

"Heath?" He looked up, and when those amazingly blue eyes connected with hers, she debated whether to share what she was feeling or keep it to herself. She'd been burned by her emotions often enough to mistrust them, but this was different. This was Heath.

So she gulped down her misgivings and charged ahead. "I just wanted to say that you've been really great, and my life got better the day we met."

Something she couldn't quite pin down warmed his gaze, making her feel like they were the only two people in the crowded room. Even though he must know people were watching them, he took her hand, threading his fingers through hers in an intimate gesture. "I feel the same way about you."

To her, this felt much more serious than their lighthearted crush conversation at the diner. As they stared at each other, she wasn't sure what had just happened, but she had a feeling things between them would never again be the way they were yesterday. And to her astonishment, she realized that was totally fine with her.

The feel of his hand grasping hers anchored her exactly the way she needed right now, so she held on as she rested her cheek on his shoulder and closed her tired, gritty eyes. She'd begun to doze off when she heard quick footsteps coming toward the waiting room. It was Paul, and just like that, she bolted upright, wide awake again.

Her cousin's long, harrowing night had left him looking exhausted, but a joyful look brightened his haggard features. Without delay, he announced, "The C-section went well, and everyone's doing great." Holding out his phone, he smiled proudly at the screen before turning it for them all to see. "I'd like you to meet Aubrey Rose Barrett."

The suddenly energized group all cheered, and despite his fatigue, Paul somehow managed to stand up under a barrage of hugs and enthusiastic backslaps. "Chelsea wants to see all of you, but it's gonna be a little while before she's ready for company. She said to tell you if you'd rather head home, she'll be just as glad to have visitors tomorrow."

"None of us have to go anywhere, honey," Olivia declared confidently. "Tell Chelsea we love her and we'll wait right here until you come back to get us."

Paul chuckled. "That's what I told her, but you know how she is."

Thinking of others, Tess added silently. Even though the woman had been through such a heart-wrenching ordeal, it would be completely understandable if she chose to send them home and get a good night's sleep instead. Tess had witnessed that kind of selfless behavior from other residents of this close-knit community, and she recognized that it was the major reason why she felt so comfortable here.

Looking around her, she saw a circle of

down-to-earth people who treasured each other but didn't care much about money. The contrast with her own upbringing was so stark, she finally understood why her father had turned his back on his humble roots. He'd wanted more luxury and had understood that he would never find it here. She felt exactly the opposite and couldn't help wondering if as he grew older, he might wish he'd taken the other path.

Chances were she'd never work up the courage to ask him that, so she'd never know the answer. She put the pointless thought out of her mind and sent up a heartfelt prayer of thanks for the divine help her family had received tonight. Her own experience had taught her how fragile a new life was, and she was grateful this little one had been strong enough to make it through her difficult birth.

Paul accepted another round of hugs and promised to return as soon as the doctor gave Chelsea the thumbs-up for visitors.

Once he was gone, Heath turned to Tess, his eyes clouded with sympathy. "You okay?"

"Of course. Why?"

"You've been worried about Chelsea losing the baby all along, so tonight must've been real hard for you."

That he'd picked up on her emotions was

stunning enough. That he'd purposefully bring up such a delicate issue only proved how fearless he truly was. Other men she'd been involved with avoided confronting a woman's feelings like the plague. But not Heath, she mused with a little smile.

Resting a hand on one rough cheek, she stood on tiptoe to kiss the other. "That's very sweet of you, but I'm fine. Just a little tired."

"Yeah," he agreed with a yawn. "I know what you mean."

"You don't have to stay. Gram drove in with Jason and Amy, so I can catch a ride home with them."

"Not a chance. I've been waiting for months to meet that little girl, and I'm not gonna miss out on seeing her just 'cause I'm a little bushed. That's why that Colombian guy with the donkey invented coffee."

She was pretty sure he had his facts wrong, but she couldn't help smiling because she knew that was what he'd been after when he made the joke. Heath wasn't a Barrett, and she marveled at the unyielding loyalty he felt to her family. He'd shown it countless times over the past several weeks, and while it no longer baffled her, she still thought it was pretty amazing.

"Sounds good to me," she commented, smothering a yawn of her own. "Let's go find some. I'm sure everyone would appreciate a boost right about now."

"We passed a coffee shop on our way here." Pulling out his phone, he punched a few keys and grinned like a kid who'd aced a tough exam. "They're open twenty-four hours. What say we grab some orders and head over there?"

She loved the way he included her in his plan, and she held up her hand for a high five. "Deal."

## Chapter Eleven

"No, Mom, I haven't changed my mind. I'm staying here for Thanksgiving."

That was the ominous phrase that greeted Heath when he arrived at the mill one cloudy November afternoon to look over yet another balky piece of machinery. Paul had decided to invoke his owner's privilege and stay home on paternity leave for a couple of weeks. While out running some errands the other day, he'd stopped by the sawmill and left strict orders for his foreman Ike Donaldson to call him if anything needed his attention.

Scott and Jason had vetoed that almost immediately, and there was a stern code of silence among the crew about broadcasting any issues that might arise and threaten their holiday delivery schedule. According to Tess, they encountered at least one major problem and three minor ones a day, but so far they'd been able to handle them and keep Paul mercifully in the dark. Heath's mission was to make sure it stayed that way.

"I know it's next week," Tess continued in an overly patient tone, "but this is the busiest time of year for the business." She paused then said, "We talked about Christmas when I called you a couple weeks ago. I'm not going to meet you and your friends in Maui or anywhere else. Traveling out from the East Coast can be a nightmare that time of year, with them canceling flights for bad weather and all."

Heath was dying to talk to her, but he felt awkward listening in, so he raised a hand to say hello on his way to the saw room. In response, she motioned for him to wait and circled her finger in the air to let him know she was almost done.

"I'm sorry you're disappointed, but I'm sure you and your friends will have a fabulous time soaking up the sun. I'll call you again soon."

Her mother was still talking when Tess switched off her phone, and Heath scowled. "That was kinda rude, don't you think?"

"I've been on the phone with her for the last hour," Tess informed him curtly. "Which apparently was happy hour for her, because she repeated some of what she was saying word for word at least three times."

Glancing at the schoolhouse clock on the wall, he frowned. "It's one o'clock in California."

"Tell me about it. That's what happens when you count on someone else to take care of you and he goes *poof*." Adding a sour look, she propped her elbows on her desk and rested her chin on her folded hands. "Over the past few years, Dad's kept finding ways to extend his trips so he's been around less and less. Even when he was there more often, she always decorated the holidays with martinis. It's depressing, and I'm not suffering through that kind of drama anymore. If that makes me a bad daughter, I'll have to live with that."

"Is that what she told you?" It didn't strike him as a very motherly thing to do, but out of respect for Tess, he managed to keep that assessment to himself.

"In those exact terms. My brothers are keeping their distance from her, to protect their wives and children from all her tantrums. So I'm all she's got left, and she unloads on me."

The dejected slump of Tess's shoulders was nothing like the strong, assertive woman he'd become so fond of. It seemed like her old life had reached out a tentacle to haul her back into the misery she'd been working so hard to leave behind, and seeing her so down made him furious.

Keeping a firm rein on his temper, he strode through the door into her office. Settling on the edge of her immaculate desk, he searched for something helpful to say. Everything he came up with sounded judgmental in his head, so he kept it simple. "I'm sorry, Tess. Is there anything I can do?"

Those dark, miserable eyes held his for a long moment, and she shook her head. When her chin started trembling, he couldn't take it anymore. Standing, he pulled her into his arms and rested her cheek on his chest. At first she kept her hands fisted on his chest, but gradually her arms slid around him and she melted against him like a child seeking comfort.

Her trusting action touched him deeply, and he strengthened his hold to let her know she wasn't alone. Words had never been his strong point, but his embrace seemed to reassure her, and her shaking gradually eased. Raising her head, she gazed up at him with a tentative smile. "Thanks, Heath."

"Anytime." With the pad of his thumb, he brushed away the last of her tears and tapped her nose. "I just don't wanna make a habit of it. No one should be that sad very often."

This smile was a bit stronger. "So, when you got here it looked like you had something to tell me. What's up?"

"Bruce called me this morning. Last night the town council approved my zoning variance for the house."

"That's awesome! Congratulations."

She added a joyful hug, and he was pleased that she could so quickly put aside her own problems and celebrate his good news. That only made the next part even more fun to share. "There's more."

"I'm not sure I can take anything else, but shoot."

"I got the house. The real estate agent called right after to say the sellers accepted my offer. The bank still has to go over everything, but I've got good credit, so it's mostly a matter of signing a lot of paperwork. The loan officer I'm working with said there's a good possibility I can move in just after Christmas."

"That's incredible," she breathed, eyes sparkling with excitement. "You couldn't ask for a better way to start the new year, could you?"

"Actually, I can."

Before he had a chance to change his mind, he leaned in to kiss her. He went slowly, to give her time to pull free of him if that was what she wanted. But she didn't.

In fact, when he broke the kiss, she pulled him back in for a longer one. Sharing that moment with her felt so right to him, he could have gone on like that forever. But if someone saw them, he knew their very personal encounter would be common knowledge around town before noon. And if that someone was Scott, he'd never live it down.

Breaking away, he gazed down at her in amazement. "Wow."

"I'm sure you say that to all the girls," she teased, mischief dancing in the eyes that had been filled with tears only a few minutes ago.

"Nope. Just you." He knew he must be grinning like a lovestruck fool, but he couldn't help himself. Didn't particularly want to, either.

Still circled in his arms, she tilted her head with that curious expression he'd come to both admire and dread. "So what happens with us now?"

"What do you want to happen?"

"Oh, you're good," she said with a quick laugh. "Is that one of your best lines?"

The glimpse of her old cynicism wasn't flattering, but considering the difficult conversation she'd had with her mother, he did his best to look past it. "It's the truth. What I want doesn't mean much if you want something else."

She gave him a thoughtful look then took his hand and tugged him out to the porch where they could get some privacy. Glancing around, she said, "I haven't told anyone in the family yet, but I'm seriously thinking about sticking around."

His heart leapt, but he firmly tamped it down to avoid being disappointed. "You mean, past the end of the year?"

"I mean, permanently. When I was over there yesterday, Chelsea said she'd love to stay home with Aubrey for a few months, and maybe work part-time after that. Now that I know how this place functions, if I was here to keep everything running smoothly, sharing the job could work for both of us. Plus, that would give me time to take a marketing class or two, either at the community college or online."

Heath knew just how important her independence was to her, and hearing her talk about her future in such concrete terms was fantastic. It also gave him hope that she might find a place in that future for him. "That's a great plan, but this town's pretty mellow most of the year. Are you sure you can handle all that quiet?"

"I get more attached to Barrett's Mill all the time. I love the scenery and the people and all the sweet, homey stuff that goes on here every day. I'm not sure I want to give all that up to go somewhere else." Giving him an urgent look, she added, "What do you think?"

This time he didn't care who saw them. He swept her up into his arms for a long kiss, pouring into it every ounce of emotion her news had unleashed in him. With her feet still several inches off the porch, he grinned at this beautiful, maddening city girl who'd started out as a thorn in his side and had become the woman he'd been searching for all these years.

"I think it's awesome."

After kissing Tess, the rest of his morning had been a bit of a blur, but one thing Heath knew for sure—he'd never been covered in this much oil. Fortunately, he'd had the foresight to put a full set of coveralls on over his clothes. His boots were another story, though. To avoid tracking grease and sawdust through the mill house's tidy reception area, he ducked out the loading dock door and jumped from the landing to the ground. Out of well-ingrained habit he always carried cleaning solution in his truck, so he headed that way.

He stripped off his filthy coveralls and started scrubbing away the worst of the mess that had soaked through them onto his skin. He was about halfway through when he heard voices and glanced into the side yard where the crew unloaded incoming salvaged logs from trucks and sorted them by species.

Tess was standing in front of a piece of aged timber that had been ripped in half lengthwise but was still nearly as tall as she was. "Everything is produced onsite by our sawyers and carpenters, using nothing but legacy equipment," she was explaining to a guy in business attire who appeared to be taking notes. "The property goes back to just after the Civil War, when Jedediah Barrett settled here after serving with Robert E. Lee in the Army of Northern Virginia. When he saw the shape this area was in, it occurred to him that there would be a lot of rebuilding going on around here and no sawmill to provide the lumber."

"And your family's been in this spot ever since? Remarkable."

Being a guy himself, Heath recognized that the comment wasn't aimed at the Barrett family as much as Tess herself. The man's voice sounded vaguely familiar, and Heath edged around to get a look at his face. When he recognized Tyler Green, the Donaldsons' accomplished—and flirtatious—nephew, Heath's hackles rose to full alert.

Ignoring the reason he'd come out here in the first place, he strolled over to reintroduce himself to the well-dressed freelancer. "Hey, Tyler. What brings you back here?"

Tyler looked surprised to see him there but hid his reaction with a quick smile. "A job. Tess asked me to do a proposal regarding some promotional work for the mill, and I couldn't resist."

The job or Tess? Heath was dying to ask. Instead, he said, "Yeah, she's tough to say no to. I don't remember you mentioning this idea to anyone," he added with a sharp look at her.

"It's a surprise. Tyler can get us national exposure through his network of contacts, and I think we should hire him to do a layout for us. It's just the thing we need to fill in that dip in sales we were expecting to have between the holidays and next summer's tourist season."

The pride in her voice told him she had no clue that skirting around Paul and Chelsea was the worst thing she could possibly do. While he was trying to come up with a subtle way to point out her error in judgment, Tyler rushed in and ambushed him.

"We've already got things moving," the ad man explained, offering Heath the slim digital tablet he'd been scribbling on. When Heath held up his filthy palms, Tyler didn't seem fazed in the least. He spun the display and steadied it so Heath could get a better look at what they'd been concocting.

Hardly larger than the last book he'd read, the screen was filled with a splashy rendering of the old mill, with the creek in the foreground and "The Sawmill" rippling through the water in a flowing script apparently intended to mimic the current. He knew next to nothing about graphic design, but to Heath it looked like Tyler had taken a picture and used some program or other to doctor the photo and make it look like an abstract painting. Tyler tapped one of the links, and the view shifted to the outer yard, highlighting the deadly-looking saw Heath was more than slightly afraid of.

"This is just a start, of course, to give you an idea of how the eventual site would be configured," Tyler explained in a polished tone that Heath suspected he'd rehearsed for use on his other clients. "We want to make sure we spotlight the most unique aspects of the business so people will remember it. Artwork like this will go a long way to setting the company apart from the competition."

"The name is 'Barrett's Sawmill,'" Heath said, irked by being forced to state the obvious.

"To compete in bigger markets, this organization needs a fresh, new approach to just about everything it does. In my world, names are changed frequently for any number of reasons."

Offended, Heath bristled at the designer's condescending manner. Being more of a hands-on kind of guy, he might not be all that familiar with advertising, but he knew a hard sell when he heard one. Looking over their guest's shoulder, he appealed to Tess. "Around here, things pretty much stay the same."

"Including our flat bottom line," she retorted in a clipped voice that warned him in no uncertain terms to back off and let the matter drop.

The mill didn't belong to him, Heath reasoned, and that meant this wasn't his fight. But he was fairly certain that if the rest of the Barretts knew what was being discussed here, they'd put on the brakes in a heartbeat.

Hoping to end up with the same result without embarrassing Tess, he approached the delicate task carefully. "You've put in quite a bit of work on this project already, Tyler. Your time must be pretty valuable."

"My consultations are free of charge. Most of the clients I meet with sign on when they see for themselves how much my team can do for their company."

So much for that tactic. Diplomacy was obviously not Heath's strong point, so he went with something a bit more direct. Turning to Tess, he asked, "What'd Paul say when you floated this past him?"

"I told you," she huffed impatiently. "I want it to be a surprise."

"Sure, 'cause you don't wanna hear what a bad idea this is." He got the distinct impression that she was being intentionally difficult, and his temper was starting to simmer. Before their disagreement had a chance to snowball into an all-out fight, he stepped forward and quietly said, "Can I talk to you a minute?"

"You two go ahead," Tyler answered smoothly before she could say anything. "I'll just grab some inside photos and ideas for the print layout."

"Thanks so much, Tyler," she replied with what Heath deemed an overly friendly smile. "This shouldn't take very long. I'll be there in a sec."

When he was out of earshot, she wheeled on Heath with a stormy expression. "What on earth is your problem?"

"I should be asking you the same thing," he countered, folding his arms in a stubborn gesture. "You're trying to make this into one of those glitzy stores folks go to and pay way more than they should because they think the stuff's handmade. This furniture—" he pointed at the mill "—is custom from the floor up. It's not a slick marketing scheme cooked up by some Ivy Leaguer who doesn't know a socket from a screwdriver."

After a couple seconds, she gave him one of those superior feminine looks any man worth his salt knew meant trouble. "You're jealous."

"Of what?"

"Tyler. He's good-looking and successful, and he has some fabulous ideas for taking this place from being a local attraction to competing in a national market."

"We have that already, with the online orders. Chelsea set up the website with a nice, rustic look that tells folks what this place is all about. The pictures are real and the descriptions are honest. People know that what they're getting is solid custom furniture made the old-fashioned way."

"What she did is very nice, but it's not enough to grow the business," Tess explained in a patient tone that made him feel like a four-year-old. "After the holidays, all the part-time workers get laid off, and they don't get hired back until we need to restock for the summer tourist season. A campaign like this will help us even out the cash flow throughout the entire year."

"Did you ever consider that those folks

wanna have some time off to go fishing and camping with their families instead of working more?"

"Don't be ridiculous," she scoffed. "They can still take a vacation to get away. But more hours here means they'll make better money, and who doesn't want that?"

Heath stared at her, stunned beyond words. His father would call it flabbergasted, he knew, but that didn't help him process what he'd just heard coming from the lips of the woman he'd begun to think might actually be "the one."

"You really believe that?" he asked, giving her a chance to reevaluate her position and see where she'd gone astray.

She gave him a look that made it plain she was baffled by his lack of understanding. "Most people do."

"I'm not asking them. I'm asking you."

"Well, then, yes, I believe that. Part of the reason I want to stay here is to help make the mill more profitable. A more consistent income will mean less worry for everyone, including Paul and Chelsea. They have their own family to think about now, and that kind of security would mean a lot to them."

"True enough, but there's more to it than that." Heath could tell his attempt at logic wasn't making a dent with her. Nearly out of options, he switched to a more personal tack. "Do you remember me telling you this place isn't about the bottom line?"

Flashing an impatient look at the mill house where Tyler was waiting for her, she sighed. "I guess I remember something like that."

"It's about tradition," he repeated as patiently as he could manage. "And your family's legacy. Now does it sound familiar?"

She didn't respond, but the dark glare she nailed him with let him know he'd finally gotten through to her. "What's your point?"

"Tyler's plan might make sense for other businesses, but not this one. Once he finds out what's going on, Paul's gonna pull rank on you and put a stop to it. As good as your intentions are, he'll never let you or anyone else destroy the character of this place. It meant too much to Will."

"I'm trying to make it stronger," she insisted, her eyes pleading with him to see her side. "Don't you understand?"

"No, I don't. But I'll tell you what's real clear to me right now." Pausing, he thought once more before he said something he'd regret. Then again, it was the truth, and his gut was telling him she needed to hear it. Even though she'd probably hate him for it. "You keep telling me how different you are from your family in California. How they're shallow and obsessed with their image instead of valuing what matters most."

"That's right. Money's the most important thing to them."

After a deep breath, he braced himself and forged ahead. "From where I'm standing, you look just like 'em."

With that, he stalked away from her and climbed into his truck, his heart as near to broken as it had ever been. Not wanting to see her reaction, he pulled around the far side of the mill house and drove up the lane to the highway.

After getting so much fantastic news this morning, he'd been looking forward to celebrating the holidays with Tess. He'd envisioned explaining football to her on Thanksgiving and had even started pondering what he could give her for Christmas.

Now he wanted nothing more than to sink himself into his new business and forget he'd ever met her. If only it was that easy.

Who did Heath Weatherby think he was, anyway?

Furious and exasperated beyond words, Tess had managed to keep her composure and finish her session with Tyler as gracefully as she could. His quick wrap-up and promise to contact her next week was a professional red flag. He hadn't mentioned it directly, but only a complete idiot could have missed her swift turn of mood from enthusiastic to one step short of homicidal.

After walking him out, she returned to the office and pounded invoices with her *Paid* stamp with more vigor than was strictly necessary. The slamming sound and bright red ink suited her current frame of mind perfectly, and she was sorry when the pile was gone. Unfortunately, her anger was still humming, and she snatched some blank paper from the printer so she could keep going.

"Is this a bad time?"

Hearing Jenna's voice, Tess didn't even bother to look up. "Yes."

"Do you want me to come back later?"

"Don't care." Realizing she sounded like a pouting toddler, Tess paused in midstamp and gave her friend a frustrated look. "Men are such a pain."

"Tell me about it." Sprawling out on the old settee by the window, Jenna grinned over at her. "Seriously, tell me. Scott and Jason are dying of thirst back there, but they're afraid to come out front to get some water."

"How do you know that?" Jenna held up her

cell phone, and Tess realized Scott must have texted his wife with an SOS. "What a couple of babies."

"Never underestimate a Barrett in full temper. Even bears cross the road to avoid Scott in the morning." Jenna's icy blue eyes crackled with humor, making it clear she wasn't the least bit intimidated by Tess's shifting moods, no matter how nasty they happened to be.

"You'd think they'd be able to take it, then."

"Sure, but when the shots are aimed at them, they crumble. Why do you think all those big, strapping men are still afraid of their mom?"

"I see what you mean," Tess conceded with a sigh. When her cousins appeared in the wide doorway that led to the saws, she waved them through. "Storm's over. Come on in."

"You're sure?" Jason asked. When she nodded, he made a beeline for the fridge in the seating area. "Man, and I thought Amy had a bad side."

"Oo, I'm telling," Jenna teased. When he glowered at her, she stuck her tongue out in reply. "We Barrett women have to stick together. You guys outnumber us, so it's our only chance."

Scott caught the water bottle Jason tossed him and grinned over at his wife. "Only 'cause we let you think you have a chance. If we ever gang up on you, you're toast."

"You'd have to agree on something first," Tess chimed in, enjoying the distraction from her dust-up with Heath. It had shaken her more than she cared to admit, and she wasn't quite sure what to do about it. Their sweet encounter that morning was a distant memory, and now that she'd had time to simmer down, she wished there was a way to rewind her day to that moment and erase all the bad stuff that had come later.

"She's got a point there," Jason acknowledged as they headed back through the door. Tess assumed the screeching slam that followed was Scott's way of ending their argument.

Turning to her guest, she shook her head. "How do you put up with him, anyway?"

"Oh, he's got his good points and bad points, just like anyone else. Are you gonna tell me what happened with Heath, or do I get to play twenty questions?"

Tess suspected it wouldn't take Jenna long to figure out the gist for herself, so she decided it was best to come clean. After she'd nutshelled the problem, she asked, "What do you think?"

"I think you're leaving something out. Like

what were you thinking, inviting Tyler Green, of all people, to do this job?"

"What do you mean *of all people*? Tyler's company does excellent work, for plenty of clients much bigger than us. The rate he quoted was a bargain considering how much they do."

"The rate he quoted *you*," Jenna commented with obvious disdain. "I'm sure he gave you the I'd-like-to-date-you number."

Jenna had traveled all over the country and met hundreds of people, some nice and others not so much. Still, Tess was shocked by her friend's cynicism. "It wasn't like that at all."

"Really? You didn't ask yourself why a guy who does promo for big-time sports teams made a detour back through teeny, tiny Barrett's Mill on his way to his swanky high-rise office in Chicago?"

"Well, no," Tess admitted, feeling more than a little foolish that she hadn't put his motives together for herself. "He seemed interested in the mill, not me."

"Don't blame yourself. He's in advertising, and he creates illusions for a living. If you ask me, Heath saw what was going on and wasn't having any of it. He's crazy about you, Tess, and it'd make him nuts to think someone like Tyler was working you over."

That was only half of the problem, Tess

recognized, but she wasn't ready to confide the rest to anyone. Because while Jenna had been setting her straight, she'd been rolling what Heath had said around in her head. She still didn't appreciate most of it, but her calmer perspective made it possible for her to understand what he'd been trying so desperately to warn her about.

Only when that had failed had he gotten tough. He'd always been so good to her that it had caught her off guard, and her knee-jerk reaction had been to snarl back and defend what she honestly felt was a viable strategy for putting the family business on sturdier financial ground.

She knew that if anyone would see her point of view, it would be the very pragmatic woman sitting across from her. "Can I ask your opinion on something?"

"Shoot."

She outlined the promotional campaign she and Tyler had discussed then showed Jenna the graphics he'd printed out for her before leaving. Giving them a cursory glance, she frowned over at Tess. "Change the name? Are you insane?"

"It was just an idea." Jenna's harsh reaction mirrored Heath's, and Tess was beginning to wonder if she was in the wrong on this one. "We don't have to do it."

Standing, Jenna crumpled the paper in her fist and made an overhead shot into the recycling bin. "You shouldn't do any of this. And if you're smart, you'll make sure Paul never hears about what went on today."

Having delivered her verdict, the normally chipper artist spun on her paint-spattered sneakers and headed for the exit. When the screen door banged shut behind her, Tess was left alone to ponder the very real possibility that not only had Tyler Green played her, she'd also come dangerously close to making a horrible business decision. Obviously, Paul had veto power on anything she proposed, but if Jenna and Heath were right, Tess would have risked losing her cousin's respect. These days that meant more to her than anything.

Feeling more than a little unnerved by what had gone on, she wandered over to peer out the front window, hoping to find something to get her grounded again. The view calmed her almost instantly, and she glanced over at the venerable old mill truck in its customary parking spot under a nearly bare oak tree.

In her memory, she heard Heath's voice: *Around here, things pretty much stay the same.*

Feeling antsy, she walked out onto the front

porch for some fresh air. She let her gaze travel through the yard to the meandering creek, where she picked up the faint trail Boyd took when he loped upstream to visit Jenna at her studio. The boys had hit a lull in their sawing, and the air around her took on a tranquil quality she'd only ever experienced out here in the woods.

Granddad's woods.

The place he'd loved so much, he'd treasured the property like it was part of the family. Worth protecting, worth fighting for. And if she'd gotten her way, she would have invited the modern world into this peaceful place— for what? Money.

"I'm sorry, Granddad," she murmured, ashamed of her lapse in judgment. "It won't happen again."

A gentle breeze sighed through the branches overhead, rustling the leaves on its way past. It ruffled her bangs, and if she hadn't known better, she'd have thought someone had kissed her forehead in forgiveness. A few months ago she would never have entertained the idea that someone could reach down from Heaven and comfort her. But with her newfound faith growing stronger every day, it seemed entirely plausible to her now.

Thanks to Heath.

That thought led to another, less appealing one, and she considered it for a few minutes before making her decision. After letting the boys know she was leaving for the day, she trudged out to the mill truck and climbed inside. As she settled into the driver's seat and turned the key, she grudgingly admitted that she'd come dangerously close to being no better than people she criticized for their blind ambition. But there was one important difference.

Heath had been there for her when she went astray, armed with the courage to yank her back on course. If nothing else, she owed him her thanks. If he'd speak to her, that is.

Morgan's Garage was closed, and Heath's distinctive truck wasn't parked at his parents' house. There was a note on the back door, and she got out to read it.

*Gone fishing. Back whenever.*

"I don't think so," Tess muttered, punching in the speed dial for Scott's number. When he answered, she didn't waste time with small talk. "Where does Heath like to fish?"

"Yeah...I don't think he'd appreciate you tracking him down just now. See, when a guy wants you to know where he is, he leaves you a map."

"He told you what happened."

"Jenna did," Scott corrected her in a tone

that clearly said he agreed with his wife. "I haven't heard from Heath since he stormed outta here earlier. What'd you say to him, anyway?"

"Things I shouldn't have, and I need to apologize." This situation had spiraled far out of her control, and she was starting to panic. The most wonderful man she'd ever met had bolted, and it didn't take a genius to figure out she was the reason. "Please, Scott. This is important."

"Why?"

"What do you mean, why? Because I feel awful and I need to tell him so."

"Why?"

Instinct told her he was getting at something, but she didn't have the patience to play this game with him. "Why are you giving me such a hard time about this?"

"Heath's been my best friend since kindergarten," he explained. "He obviously wants to be alone right now, and I'm not giving him up unless you have a real good reason."

"Fine." Realizing she had no choice, she blew out a frustrated breath and 'fessed up. "I don't want him to hate me."

"Because?"

"Oh, give the poor girl a break," Jenna chided him. "She was wrong and wants to go make it right. Just tell her how to find him."

"Scott! You're supposed to let someone know when they're on speaker."

"My bad. Tessie, you're on speaker."

Laughter piped through the phone and rather than battle them both, Tess joined in. "You're hilarious. Wait till I tell Gram."

That got her a warning growl from her irritable cousin. "Do you want accurate directions, or do you want to end up in a no-name swamp somewhere?"

"Sorry. Go ahead."

"Heath's dad has a hunting cabin on Hoover Lake. You take the highway west, but when you pull off the main road it gets complicated. Got a pen?"

Clearly, there were no fish left in this lake.

Sitting on the dock outside the rustic log cabin he and his father had built years ago, Heath scowled at the mirror-calm water. No ripples meant no fish, even though he'd caught the flash of more than one trout off to either side of him. Maybe they sensed his dark mood and were keeping their distance. Smart fish.

Only this morning, he'd been sailing along without a cloud in sight. He had a job he loved, a house in escrow and the town's stamp of approval for his garage plans. The work he'd been doing at the mill was holding up well, and the crew was ramping up production for the all-important holiday season.

And he had Tess.

When she told him she was thinking about staying in Barrett's Mill, he'd felt as if he'd found the final piece of the puzzle that would complete his future. His new house wasn't far from Scott and Jenna's, and more than once he'd envisioned the four of them hanging out together. Helping each other with projects, raising their kids together, enjoying the kind of life his parents' happiness had encouraged him to aim for.

Raising his line, he frowned at the empty hook dangling from the end. It glittered in the sunlight, and he felt like it was mocking him for not paying close enough attention to what he was doing. That's what happened when he thought about Tess, he recognized with a sigh. Everything else faded into the background because quite simply, nothing compared to her.

Even when she was wrong, she was still the most incredible woman he'd ever known. A baffling, strong-willed handful, today wasn't the first time he'd asked himself what he saw in her. Despite their bitter argument, in his heart he knew she was still the woman he'd joyfully swept into his arms that morning. He just wished he knew how to reclaim that feeling.

"Permission to come aboard?"

Startled by the sound of her voice, Heath dropped his fishing rod in the water and whirled to find her standing behind him. Tilting her head, she said, "I'm not a fisherman, but I think you're supposed to hang on to the pole or the fish get away."

"Yeah, I guess so." Remembering the manners Mom had drummed into him since childhood, he stood and faced his unexpected guest. "How'd you find me?"

"Scott. He made me promise to tell you—hang on." Flipping open a folded set of handwritten directions, she cleared her throat. "'Jenna made me do it. And if Heath gets mad and tosses you in the lake, you got this map from Jason.'"

Heath chuckled. "That sounds like him. So why did his wife make him give you directions to drive out here?"

Just like that, her expression dimmed, and Tess fixed him with a somber look. "I want to apologize for what happened at the mill earlier. I wasn't thinking straight, and when you pointed that out, I turned on you."

"Like a rattlesnake. How come?"

Glancing around at the placid surroundings, she came back to him with a shrug. "You were telling me something I didn't want to hear."

"You wanted me to say how brilliant you were?" Hoping to lighten the mood, he tipped his head with a little grin.

"Something like that."

His attempt at humor had done nothing to ease the tension snapping in the air between them, so he tried again. "You *are* brilliant, Tess. Just not always right." Scowling, she opened her mouth but he beat her to the punch. "No one is. I'm sorry I came down so hard on you. You're not the least bit heartless, and I had no business saying otherwise."

"You must have had a reason." Taking a step closer, she gazed up at him with curiosity lighting her eyes. "What was it?"

It had nothing to do with the mill, he'd come to realize once his temper cooled. While he cared deeply about what happened to the iconic landmark, concern for the property was only part of the answer to her question.

Taking a deep breath, he readied himself for some good, old-fashioned ridicule. "Tyler."

"I'm gonna need more than that."

"I didn't like the way he was eyeballing you at church," Heath explained, "and it was ten times worse today. I don't trust the guy."

"You don't even know him," she pointed out with a short laugh.

"I know guys like him and so do you. I can't figure out what you see in him, is all."

Taking another step, she stopped so she was within arm's reach. Reaching a hand to his cheek, she bathed him in the most beautiful smile he'd ever seen. "I don't see half of what I see in you, Heath. Does that make you feel better?"

In reply, he lifted her up for a long, joyful kiss. When he broke away, she gave him a little smirk. "Does that mean I'm forgiven?"

"Oh, yeah."

"I'm still learning what's really important in life, Heath. I hope you won't give up on me while I'm working on it."

"I think we can figure something out."

Setting her on her feet, he kept her circled in his arms. Framing her face in his hands, he leaned in for a long, gentle kiss that came pretty close to buckling her knees.

Once she regained some of her senses, she blinked up at him. "What was that for?"

He shrugged, then gave her a look she'd never seen from him before. She'd assumed she'd seen them all by now, but this one had a special quality to it that warned her something was going on.

"'Cause I love you."

It was a good thing he was holding her, or she'd have dropped from shock. Slowly shaking her head, she stammered, "No, you don't."

"Yeah, I do." The corner of his mouth crooked into an aggravating male smirk, and he said, "I'm not sure why, but I do."

"Seriously?" she huffed in exasperation. "You don't know why you love me?"

"Hey, it's not so crazy. You don't know why you love me."

"I don't l—"

Completely against her will, the protest ended abruptly as if some unseen hand had been clamped over her mouth. Tess tried to restart her brain and finish the sentence, but something stopped her. After a few panicky moments, she understood what it was.

Her heart.

It seemed to have taken over, shoving logic into the background and allowing her normally restrained emotions to take center stage. Despite her usual reserve, she felt herself responding to the warmth in Heath's eyes in a way she'd never experienced with anyone else.

"You're right," she murmured, hardly daring to believe it. "I do love you. How on earth did you know when I didn't?"

He gave her a long, assessing look. "Have you ever loved anyone?"

"I was engaged, remember?"

"Sure, but were you in love with Avery, or did you love him? There's a difference."

"Semantics," she declared with a wave of her hand. "Love is love."

"Really? Are you sure about that?"

They were so close, he could have easily kissed her again. But he didn't. Instead, his face hovered just beyond reach, and she caught the scent of soap mixed with sawdust from the mill. Better than the priciest cologne, she knew that for the rest of her life, whenever she smelled that combination, she'd think of this country boy with the quick smile and the generous heart.

Avery would continue to fade from her memory until she could barely recall his face. In contrast, Heath was branded there, and in a flash of epiphany, she understood why.

God intended for him to be there.

In His wisdom, He'd recognized what Tess needed most and directed her steps to where she'd be sure to find it. Heath was strong and solid, confident enough to let her stand on her own but be close by if she needed him. That was what he meant to her, why her feelings for him had grown into something she'd never anticipated.

"Now that you mention it, I'm not sure at all."

She punctuated that with a little grin, and he chuckled. "Are you trying to tell me something?"

"I'm trying to tell you I love you, too. How does that sound?"

"Pretty amazing."

He laced his fingers through hers and dropped a kiss on the back of her hand. The romantic gesture was so at odds with his rugged appearance, she couldn't believe one man managed them both so well. Then he reached up and tucked her hair behind her ear with such a gentle touch, it took everything she had not to sigh like a teenager with her first crush.

Strong, gentle and kind, she thought dreamily. And a treat to look at, besides. What more could a girl ask for?

# Chapter Twelve

"Really? Everything's a go?" Straining to control his excitement, Heath just about crushed his cell phone to keep from letting out a yelp of joy. It was the day before Thanksgiving, and the holiday had just taken on a whole new meaning for him. "Thank you very much. You just made my day."

The normally businesslike mortgage loan officer on the other end of the phone actually laughed. "I'm so glad to hear that. We should be able to wrap everything up the week before Christmas. The sellers' agent was in earlier and asked me to tell you that since the house is empty the owners have agreed to let you move in and pay rent for this coming month."

"That's awesome," he replied. His parents had gotten home last night, so the timing couldn't be better for him to get set up in his own place.

"Monday I'll contact your attorney with the details about the closing. Happy Thanksgiving."

"You, too."

After hanging up, the first thing he did was lower his head and close his eyes. He didn't have the words to express precisely what he was feeling, so he just kept quiet, trusting that God would get the gist.

Once he'd given his thanks, he didn't have to think about who to call first with his great news. When Tess answered, he tried to sound casual. "Whatcha doin'?"

"Clearing off my desk for the long weekend. How about you?"

"Not much. Wanna take a ride with me?"

The tightly wound woman he met a few short weeks ago would have deflected that offer with a cautious demand for more information. The caring, generous one who'd driven into the boonies to apologize to him, though, simply laughed. "Sure. I'll be ready when you get here."

"Cool. See you in ten."

Since he had a few minutes to spare, he swung by the house—his house, he amended with a grin—and admired the Sold sign that hung in place of the Pending one that had been there yesterday. Snapping a photo, he texted it to his tech-savvy mother with the caption:

*Guess you and Dad can turn my old room into a gym.*

She responded with a laughing face, and he grinned as he tossed his phone into a cup holder and headed for the mill. He'd always loved the area he grew up in, but today it struck him as being especially beautiful. His roots were here, and coming back had been the right move for him. If only Tess ended up settling here, too, his future would be everything he could possibly ask for.

When he pulled up near the mill house, something was different. At first he couldn't place it, and then it hit him. It was quiet. No voices, no equipment grinding and whirring. Instead, he heard the running creek and a few birds chirping to each other from the nests they'd made in the wide eaves. Through the bare trees, he could just make out the outline of the small garage he was planning to expand to accommodate his new business. It was even closer than he thought.

"You look happy," Tess told him as she came through the screen door. "Did Fred give you an extra day off or something?"

"Even better." He noticed her agile mind hadn't gone immediately to him getting a monetary bonus from his boss. Just another change from her old self that made him want to spend more time with her. They met on the stairs, and he paused one step below, grinning up at her. "I was planning to drive, but it's such a nice day, we could actually walk."

Glancing around, she came back to him with a quizzical look. "To where?"

"You'll see."

Holding out his hand, he was pleased when she took it without hesitation. She trusted him not to lead her into trouble, he realized. Considering the tough knock she'd taken from the last man she'd believed in, knowing she had that kind of faith in Heath made him feel incredible.

"So," he began as they started walking. "How's the Barrett Thanksgiving dinner coming along?"

"Chaos, of course. Gram and Aunt Diane have been in the kitchen most of the day, and Scott's all grumpy because we're not eating at Paul and Chelsea's. Something about the breakfront he killed himself to finish."

"There used to be a buffet in their dining room, and Chelsea wanted to replace it," Heath explained with a chuckle. "Scott's a wiz with that detailed stuff, and she asked him to have it ready by fall so she and Paul could host everyone at their place. She usually has everything under control, but she didn't plan on having Aubrey a month early."

"I think the best things happen when we forget the plan and just let things fall the way God intended." Pulling his arm around her, she cuddled in with a sweet sigh. "Like us."

He really loved the way that sounded, but he was still leery of spooking her with too much emotional stuff all at once. Instead, he brought her in closer and dropped a kiss on top of her head. "Yeah, I guess He knew what He was doing."

"Of course, Gram takes all the credit. Last night I finally got her to admit she sabotaged the truck that morning." Laughing, she shook her head. "Since it all worked out, she's proud of herself for thinking of it."

"Y'know, if you wanna keep on driving it, I could give it a new paint job and see what I can do with the chrome."

Tess drew her head back and nailed him with a warning look. "Don't you dare. I love that old beast just the way it is, rust and all."

"Spoken like a true Barrett." They'd arrived at the back edge of his property, and he stopped in the middle of a faint deer trail, grinning like a fool. "Here we are. My place."

He could tell she didn't understand what he meant. Then comprehension dawned, and her eyes widened with the same kind of excitement he'd felt earlier.

"Your mortgage got approved? Heath, that's wonderful!" After an exuberant hug, she arched back and beamed up at him. "How does it feel?"

"Amazing. Terrifying," he added with a wry grin. "That's a mighty big check to write out every month."

"Once you get Blue Ridge Classics up and running, it won't be so bad. Would you like to show me around?"

"I don't have the keys yet, but we can check out everything else. The owners said I can move in and pay them rent until we close."

"I've got a bunch of empty shipping boxes at the mill, with more coming in next week. You're welcome to as many of those as you need."

There was a real benefit to being involved with such a practical woman. She was always thinking. While that used to bother him, these days he saw it for the positive that it was. "That'd be great. Thanks."

As they strolled around the yard to the front of the house, she pointed at the huge bay window. "You could have an enormous Christmas tree right there. Garlands around the porch columns, and candles in all the windows."

"That could work."

In his experience, when a woman started decorating your place for you, she was anticipating spending a lot of time there. In past relationships, that had been a major red flag for him, but because it was Tess, somehow it just felt right. He wished she'd tell him she was staying in Barrett's Mill, but he managed to keep himself from saying so.

For too long, she'd gone along with what other people wanted, rather than doing what would be best for her. Her growing independence was a good thing, and he was proud of the strides she'd made. He'd never dream of trying to influence her on such an important choice.

But he was only human. If she eventually decided to leave, he'd miss her more than he cared to think about. Reeling her into his arms, he dropped in for a warm, leisurely kiss.

When he pulled away, he rested his forehead on hers with a sigh. "Love you."

"Love you back."

Snaking her arms around his waist, she studied him with a somber expression. He sensed she was weighing her options, trying to make the very choice he'd been dreading only a few moments ago. As they gazed at each other, her eyes darkened ominously, and he waited for her to tell him she'd come to a decision and would be leaving after Christmas.

But she didn't. Instead, she turned and headed around the side of the house. "Show me what you've got in mind for the shop."

When he didn't follow, she pivoted back to him with a confused look. "Are you coming?"

*Are you staying?* He was dying to ask, but he clamped his mouth shut and simply nodded in response to her question.

Somehow, when he wasn't looking, he'd allowed his future to become entwined with hers. While his business was on track, his personal life was in a holding pattern, waiting for her to make up her mind. From day one he'd suspected this woman had the potential to drive him to the edge of his sanity.

Today he knew it for sure.

After their little tour Heath walked Tess back to the mill. At the foot of the porch steps, he pulled her close and gave her the playful grin she'd come to adore. "I almost forgot. Mom asked me to invite you to dinner tonight. It won't be anything fancy, but they've been hearing a lot about you and wanted to meet you in person."

"I hope you told them nice things."

She put a sarcastic spin on that, hoping to

mask the rush of panic sweeping over her. Introducing a girl to your parents was the kind of thing you did when you were serious about her, but she hadn't decided whether or not she was staying in Barrett's Mill yet. One minute she thought yes, the next she worried she was limiting herself by taking the first job that had come her way. She was making herself crazy with all this hemming and hawing, but true to his patient nature, Heath hadn't made any attempt to sway her one way or the other. Quite honestly, she didn't know how he could stand it.

"I told them *every*thing." For about a second he kept a straight face then broke into a grin. "Don't worry, magpie. They're both half a bubble off plumb, and they're gonna love you."

"I'm not sure what bubbles have to do with anything, but I'll take your word for it."

"That way, you won't have to meet them for the first time tomorrow."

"Tomorrow…" Tapping her chin, she glanced up at the sky as if trying to remember what he was referring to. When he let out a mock growl, she laughed. "Oh, right. Turkey day."

"Football day," he corrected her with a quick kiss.

"About that. I have a confession to make." He cocked his head with interest, and she continued. "I know more about the game than you might think."

"Really? Why's that?"

"My dad went to UCLA, and he's a huge fan. We used to go to the games with him, and he explained everything to us in great detail. Actually," she added pensively, "it was one of the few things he and I both enjoyed."

Sympathy shone in Heath's eyes, and he frowned. "You miss him, don't you?"

"He's been traveling a lot, and I haven't seen him since Easter. He and Mom were barely speaking, so it wasn't exactly a warm, fuzzy kind of family gathering."

"You didn't answer my question."

"I know," she acknowledged with a sigh. "Mostly because I'm not sure. I mean, Mom begged me to come back, but I haven't heard a thing from him. I called and emailed, inviting him to Thanksgiving dinner, but he hasn't responded. Maybe now that he's on his own again, he decided he doesn't want a family anymore."

The last comment stuck in her throat, and she swallowed hard to keep traitorous tears from escaping her control. But Heath knew her well enough to see them, anyway, and he gathered her into his arms, resting his cheek on top of her head.

"He's going through a tough stretch right now, Tess. Give him time, and he'll come around."

"You've never even met him," she murmured against his chest. "How can you be so sure?"

Cradling her face in his strong, capable hands, he gave her an encouraging smile. "Because any man who taught his daughter to like football can't be all bad."

She let out a hiccupping laugh, and he gave her a bracing hug. "That's better. I hate to leave, but I've got a bunch of firewood to stack this afternoon. Dad's back has been bothering him, and I don't want him doing too much."

What a sweet, considerate man, Tess thought as he left her with a quick kiss and sauntered over to his truck. If she had any sense at all, she'd stop all this waffling and drop anchor in Barrett's Mill. She'd never gotten good results from listening to her gut, but this time it was telling her something that actually made sense.

Hold on to Heath Weatherby and never let him go.

But that wasn't in keeping with the self-reliant lifestyle she'd vowed to take on, she reminded herself as she went into the mill house. While she did a circuit to make sure the place was empty and everything was shut off, she let her imagination wander a little. No surprise, it ended up at the Cape Cod home upstream with the bay window and the big front yard.

The only thing missing from that picture was a family. It didn't take much to envision a tire swing dangling from one of the oak trees, a bike or two propped up in the driveway. As she locked the mill's front door, it struck her that Heath had bought a house for the wife and children he wanted but didn't currently have.

Now that was faith.

Driving along the winding road, she slowed down for a curve near the sign that read *Barrett's Mill Cemetery*. On impulse, she took the right fork and followed the lane up to the rolling acres of grass that marked the resting places of people who'd lived in this lovely little town and would always be part of its history.

There was a car in the lot, and she idly noted that it had rental plates from Maryland. Someone in for the holiday, she assumed as she parked beside it. It was nice of them to take the time to come out here and visit their relatives.

She walked up the rise and was surprised to see a man in a gray trench coat standing in the general vicinity of Granddad's grave. As she got closer, he came into clearer focus, and she hardly dared to believe he was really there.

"Dad?"

Startled eyes met hers, and he backed away from the marker like a child who'd been caught doing something wrong. "Hello, Tess."

He continued backpedaling, and she hurried forward, grasping his arms to hold him in place. He still looked anxious, and he stood stiffly when she embraced him. Pulling away from him a bit, she gave him her biggest, brightest smile. "I'm so glad to see you."

"You are?" He relaxed a bit but still looked ready to take off at the first sign of trouble. "What about the divorce? I just assumed you'd take your mother's side."

"Because I'm a girl? Please. I think there's plenty of blame to go around on that one, don't you?"

Deep circles shadowed his eyes, telling her the last few months had taken a serious toll on him. But now a tentative smile lightened his features enough for her to see that he'd made the right decision in ending his failed marriage. "I suppose so. I never expected you kids to understand that, though."

"I'm starting to," she said, doing her best to sound upbeat. Now that she'd gotten to know the family who'd raised him, she saw the contradiction between what he'd grown up with and what he and Mom had created in California. The difference was sobering, to say the least.

He stared down at his father's grave with a frown. "Dad never could, and now it's too late to tell him he was right."

"About what?"

Grimacing, he hung his head before looking at her. "Your mother and I met in college, and I brought her home to meet my parents. Dad took me aside and warned me not to marry her. He said she wasn't the kind of girl I needed, and I'd do better to keep looking. Obviously, I didn't listen."

"That's why you never came back," Tess filled in the blank for him. "You didn't want him to see how unhappy you were."

"I really hate being wrong."

Boy, could she relate to that. Lately, though, she'd evolved a new perspective on that issue. Being wrong wasn't the problem. Obstinately denying the truth was, especially when it hurt you and the people you loved.

"Don't you think he knew?" She got a sharp look and hurried on. "I mean, he was your father, and he probably knew you better than anyone. Isn't it reasonable to assume he put the pieces together on his own?"

"Then why didn't he tell me?"

"Because he was as stubborn as you are,"

she shot back with a chiding look. "I'm finding out that's a family trait. Apparently, it comes with the brown eyes."

To her astonishment, he chuckled and shook his head. The reaction reminded her distinctly of her uncle Tom, and she felt a tug of empathy for this strong-willed man who'd come to his senses too late to mend fences with his father.

Tucking her arm through his, she drew him back to where he'd been when she found him. "Granddad's happy to see you. I know it."

He gave her a long, dubious look. "How?"

"Because that's the kind of man he was. Even if he was standing right here, he wouldn't scold you for being away so long. He'd ask how your trip was, or something like that. Right?"

His eyes fixed on the granite arch, he slowly nodded. "Yes, he would."

"You know who else is gonna be thrilled to see you? Gram. I didn't tell her I invited you for Thanksgiving, so this will be a great surprise for her."

He didn't reply at first, and it didn't take her long to figure out why. "She invited you, too, didn't she?"

"Last week. *We* were hoping to surprise *you*."

It was all too funny, and they both started laughing. But he quickly sobered. "This isn't the place for laughter, Tess."

"I don't think he minds a bit." Now it was her turn to glance at Granddad's resting place. Turning back to her dad, she added, "More than that, he'd probably think it was hilarious that we both ended up here at the same time. Isn't that strange?"

"Very. But since it gave us a chance to clear the air, I'm not going to question it." Relief flooded his tired features, and he put an arm around her shoulders and steered her toward the footpath that led to the parking lot. When he saw the mill truck, he laughed again. "That thing was ancient when I was a kid. Are your cousins playing some kind of trick on you?"

"In their dreams," she retorted with a grin. "I like driving it. It has character."

"I can't argue with that."

"Why don't you lead the way, and I'll follow you to Gram's?"

He shot her a suspicious look. "Making sure I don't turn back onto the highway and run off again?"

"Something like that."

Fortunately, he didn't argue with that, either. Her father had always been a complex man, but while they made their way through his hometown—the place she'd come to adore—some of her old quarrels with him began to fade. He'd stood up to his own father to be with the woman he loved. It hadn't worked out, but she had to give Dad credit for facing up to his mistakes and returning after so many years away. It couldn't have been easy for him to do, and she admired his courage.

They turned into the driveway, and he stepped out of his car, looking around the neighborhood where he'd spent his childhood. Glancing over at her, he seemed totally bewildered by what he'd seen. "Nothing's changed."

"Around here," she said, quoting Heath, "things pretty much stay the same."

"Except my father's gone."

Seeing the misery in his eyes, she firmly shook her head. "He's still here, watching over things, making sure the family's okay. When we keep someone in our hearts, they're never really gone."

"I'm sorry you never met him."

"So am I," she confessed with a sad smile. "But I've gotten to know him in other ways, and I think he was a really great guy."

"Yes, he was."

Her father seemed ready to say something more when the creak of a door interrupted their conversation. Wearing a ruffled bib apron, Gram shielded her eyes with a flour-covered hand and squinted into the setting sun. "Tess? Who've you got there?"

He looked over at her, and her face broke into a delighted mother's smile. "George?"

"Hello, Mom." Hands shoved deep into the pockets of his coat, he stood awkwardly rooted in place. "How have you been?"

"Missing my boy, that's how. Are you planning to stand in the driveway gawking at me, or are you coming up here for a proper greeting?"

He didn't run onto the porch, but it was pretty close. As he swept Gram into a joyful hug, tears stung Tess's eyes. She'd never been one for mushy reunions, but this one suited the day perfectly.

After all, she reasoned as she dabbed her eyes, tomorrow was Thanksgiving. And this year the Barretts had a lot to be thankful for.

Heath had been in more precarious situations. Dangling off the sheer side of a canyon came to mind, and so did scaling the arm of a disabled excavator to repair the hydraulics. But nothing he'd ever done had scared him as much as introducing Tess to his parents.

He'd never done that before, he realized while he set the table for dinner. Mom thought he was being extra helpful because she'd just gotten home, but in reality he was desperate for something to do besides watch the hands on the old mantel clock drag toward seven. That afternoon at the new house, he'd sensed a shift in Tess's usually cautious demeanor. While she hadn't come right out and said she'd made a decision about where she planned to settle, he had the feeling she was pretty close to it.

Which way would she jump? he wondered again. During the time he'd known her, he'd learned it was best not to try to predict what was going through that quick mind of hers. He loved her more than he'd once thought was possible, and he believed her when she said she loved him. Since he didn't have a choice, he was doing his best to stay light on his feet and accept whatever turn was coming his way.

But it wasn't easy.

When the doorbell sounded promptly at seven, he called out, "I'll get it!"

Setting down the last glass, he hurried into the foyer and opened the door to find her wearing the same flowered dress he'd admired at church. Smiling because he couldn't help himself, he kissed her cheek and stepped back to let her in. "Hey there. Right on time."

"Hey yourself." Moving closer, she murmured, "Could I talk to you out here a minute?"

A wave of dread hit him like a truck before he got a grip on emotions that were hovering dangerously close to the surface. Trying to mask his reaction, he joked, "That depends. Am I gonna like what you have to say?"

In response, she gave him a siren's smile and grabbed his arm to tug him out onto the porch. After following that up with a long, luscious kiss, she gazed up at him with joy glittering in her dark eyes. "I'm staying in Barrett's Mill."

Spinning her into a twirl, he kissed her soundly before putting her down. Studying her carefully, he searched for some sign that she'd spoken impulsively and might regret what she'd said. He saw nothing but certainty in her expression, but for his own sake, he had to be absolutely certain. "You're sure? This is really where you want to be?"

"Yes, and yes. Are you happy?"

"Very." Wrapping his arms around her, he tried to come up with some words that properly expressed what he was feeling. Like so many guys before him, Heath fell back on the three that had brought him to where he was now. "I love you."

"And I love you."

"Is that why you're staying?"

"Yes. Is that okay with you?"

The eagerness in her tone contradicted the confident, assertive woman he'd come to treasure, and he laughed. "I think I can make it work."

"By the way, you won't believe who I ran into at the cemetery this afternoon. My dad."

"That's funny, 'cause I was talking to my folks, and they remember him from high school. They'd love to see him again. You should invite him over to join us."

"I think he'd like that, too," she replied. "You're sure it's not an imposition?"

"There's always room for one more." Adding another kiss, he asked, "Are you hungry?"

"Definitely. Something smells incredible in there."

"Roast beef."

"Let me guess," she teased, "it's your favorite."

Opening the door, he chuckled. "Yeah. Mom always makes it for me when I'm home."

"Maybe after they get settled in, she can give me the recipe. And teach me how to use it," Tess added in a wry tone.

"That'd be cool. Then I'd get to eat it even more often."

"And do the dishes," she added tartly. "I'm gonna be busy with work and school, so I won't have time for all that domestic goddess stuff."

"Yes, ma'am."

While her announcement had more than a little bite to it, her genuine enthusiasm for the future softened the impact. He wasn't the greedy type, and right now the fact that she was settling in his hometown was more than enough for him.

After being awakened before dawn by the scent of fresh cinnamon rolls, Tess was occupied in Gram's kitchen, prepping side dishes and babysitting two enormous turkeys the size of emus. The house was gradually filling with family, and she shuttled between greeting new arrivals, filling Gram's silver chafing dishes and basting. Basically, she was in charge of any culinary task that didn't threaten to poison anyone, and she was enjoying the hands-on approach to a holiday that Mom had always hired caterers for.

When Tess finally had a moment to herself, she got a glass of water and stood at the window to drink it. Something in the backyard caught her attention, and she nudged the lacy curtain aside for a better look.

Heath had snuck in when she wasn't looking, and he was adding fresh firewood to Gram's neat stack beside the garage. That wasn't noteworthy, since he regularly helped out all over town with things like that. The newsflash was who he was talking to while he worked.

Her father.

Heath said something that made him laugh, and the sight of them together like that made her smile. Dad had made no secret of the fact that he was nervous about seeing his brothers and their families again after all these years. She'd been surprised to discover that, while he hadn't visited in person, he'd kept in sporadic contact with Uncle Tom, who was the youngest. So while they hadn't met her until now, the Virginia branch of the family had been aware that Tess existed.

If only she'd had the same knowledge, she thought with a sigh. Life would have been so much easier knowing she wasn't an odd sock but meant to be part of another set altogether.

Speaking of odd, it was quite the experience watching her Brooks Brothers father chatting with her flannel-and-jeans country boy. Then again, Heath could have a conversation with a post. Since she was on the uptight side, his easygoing nature was one of the things she loved most about him.

Against all logic, she'd done much more than fall in love with the bighearted mechanic. She adored him in a way she once hadn't even considered possible outside the covers of a romance novel. And if that wasn't astonishing enough, he'd made it abundantly clear that he felt the same way about her. As Heath and her father came up the back porch steps together, she couldn't imagine life getting any better.

"So what were you two doing out there?" she asked while they washed their hands at the sink.

"Debating which teams are gonna win the football games today," Heath answered, giving her a quick kiss on the cheek while he dried his hands. "What else do guys talk about on Thanksgiving?"

"Good point."

Now that her straightlaced father was back in his childhood home, she was seeing a whole new side of him. Of course, that might have something to do with the fact that she'd spent most of her life so wrapped up in her own troubles, she didn't have energy for much else. Heath had shown her another way to live, and no matter what happened between them, she'd always be grateful to him for that.

"I think I'll see if Mom needs help with the buffet," Dad said smoothly, taking a stack of dishes from the counter and into the dining room.

Tess caught the subtle wink he gave Heath on his way past, and when he was gone, she turned to Heath with narrowed eyes. "Okay, Weatherby. What's going on?"

"Whattya mean?" He flashed her the most innocent look she'd ever seen, but the mischievous twinkle in his eyes gave him away.

"You and Dad were cooking up something out there in the yard. I want to know what it was."

"I think you were imagining things," he teased, sliding his arms around her to pull her closer. "All the cooking's going on in here. We were just piling up some wood for Olivia is all."

He bent down for a kiss, but she leaned back and glared up at him. "Not until you tell me what's going on."

"Okay, fine."

His playful expression gave way to a more serious one, and she stopped him with a hand on his chest. "Wait. If it's something I won't like, it can wait. I don't want to spoil today with nasty stuff."

"Oh, I think you'll like it." Reaching into the watch pocket of his jeans, he pulled out a beautiful antique ring set with a modest diamond flanked by two smaller ones. Taking her left hand, he slid it onto her third finger and lifted it to his lips for a kiss. Returning her shocked look with a calm one of his own, he asked, "Whattya think?"

It took her a few seconds to find her voice. When she finally did, it occurred to her that he hadn't said the words she wanted—that she needed—to hear. Rather than scold him, though, she opted to deflect his mischief back to him. "It's very pretty."

That got her a confused reaction, but true to the character she'd come to value so much, he recovered quickly. Chuckling, he said, "It's been in my family a long time, and it's got a great track record. I love you, Tess, and I'm hoping you'll marry me and help me carry on the tradition."

"You're proposing to me when I'm covered in bread crumbs and turkey juice?"

"Well, yeah. Is that okay?"

It was time to put the poor guy out of his misery. Beaming up at him, she nodded. "It's perfect."

"Can I take that as a yes?"

"Yes." Drawing his face to hers, she sealed her answer with a kiss.

She nearly jumped out of her skin when applause broke out. Standing a few feet away, framed in the archway that led to the dining room, stood a crowd of people cheering as if they'd just witnessed an unexpected touchdown. Now that the private moment was over, they all surged into the kitchen, surrounding Heath and Tess in a circle of hugs, back-patting and good wishes.

"How long were you crazy people standing there?" she demanded with a laugh.

"Long enough to know I was right," Gram announced proudly. "No matter what anyone else thought, I always thought you two were a solid match."

Heath chuckled. "Have you called Helen and Lila yet to tell them?"

"Good idea. They'll spread the word for you." Patting them both on the arm, she hurried toward the living room for the phone. Pausing in the doorway, she asked, "Do you have a wedding date in mind?"

Heath angled a look at Tess, and she hesitated. "It's silly."

"I doubt that. What is it?"

"Christmas Eve," she confided shyly. "It's my favorite night of the year."

"Any objections?" he asked the family. When he got a chorus of noes, he grinned down at her. "Christmas Eve it is."

Delighted by his quick, unthinking agreement, she let out a very uncharacteristic squeal of excitement and embraced the man who'd made it all possible.

Simply by loving her. And always backing it up.

# *Epilogue*

"With this ring, I thee wed." After sliding Tess's ring onto her finger, Heath lifted her hand for a kiss. Finishing the romantic gesture with a subtle grin, he whispered, "Merry Christmas Eve, magpie."

Hearing his quirky nickname for her in such a solemn setting made her laugh. A few months ago, she couldn't have dreamed up an evening as perfect as this one had been. But here she was, taking his gold wedding band from its place on Pastor Griggs's open Bible, ready to make the commitment she'd resisted for so long. Silently, she thanked God for her country boy. Heath had found things in her she hadn't known were there, and now she couldn't imagine her life without him.

Gratitude welled inside her, and she swallowed hard to make sure her voice would come out confident and clear. Slipping his ring into place, she repeated, "With this ring, I thee wed."

Beaming proudly, Pastor Griggs pronounced them husband and wife and stepped back to let them have the spotlight for their first kiss as Mr. and Mrs. Heath Weatherby. The entire congregation burst into applause, and they turned to face the people who'd stayed beyond the traditional service to attend their wedding.

"Thanks for coming, everyone," Heath said as he put an arm around Tess's shoulders. "We hope to see you all over at Paul and Chelsea's."

Their guests cheered in response, and fifteen minutes later the stately Colonial was filled with people talking, laughing and digging into the best Barrett family feast yet.

"I have to admit," Jenna said, "getting married on Christmas Eve is pretty cool."

"Even though you had to wear a dress?" Scott teased, plucking his best man's boutonniere off the lapel of his suit jacket and tucking it into her bouquet.

"Even though. I mean, the church was pretty enough, but look at this place. Chelsea made it look like a Thomas Kinkade painting in here."

Tess couldn't argue with her matron of honor, even if she'd wanted to try. Which she didn't, since this was her wedding day and she had a smile permanently fixed to her face. The entire ground floor looked like a page out of a designer's magazine on how to decorate for the holidays. Fresh garlands tied with velvet ribbons were looped along the walls, dotted with antique ornaments every few feet.

The living room's wide front window showcased a huge spruce that held the collection of vintage decorations Chelsea had collected over the years. Some were Victorian, others were hand-painted tin and ceramic, and still others looked like they were made of spun glass. Over top of it all, a lacy angel floated in the place of honor. Tess was just giddy enough to imagine the little cherub keeping an eye on everyone to make sure they were enjoying themselves.

In the doorways hung more of the garland, with mistletoe added in the centers of the wide openings to encourage plenty of kisses. People seemed to have no reservations about putting the romantic greenery to good use, and the air was filled with a warm, loving vibe even the most talented wedding planner couldn't have come close to duplicating.

"I never would've been able to pull all this together without your help," Tess told her ruthlessly organized cousin-in-law. Ticking the red and green bow on her very junior bridesmaid's head, she smiled, too. "Or yours, Aubrey. You did a fabulous job during the ceremony."

"Slept through most of it," Paul informed her with a chuckle. "I couldn't get her to settle down no matter what I did, but your father's a natural when it comes to fussy babies."

Seeking him out in the crowded dining room, she found him standing in a masculine circle with his brothers and cousins, laughing about something or other. "Yeah, I'm learning a lot about him I never knew before."

"We all are," Paul said quietly. "It'll be nice to have him around for a couple weeks. He and Dad still have a lot of catching up to do."

He'd just finished speaking when Jason and Amy bounded over to join them. After they delivered another set of congratulatory hugs, Jason got right to the point. "What'd you guys think of the kids' Christmas pageant tonight?"

"Adorable, like always," Jenna answered. "Why?"

"Of course it was," Amy said, "but we could make it even better next year. What if—" she held up her hands in a director's framing pose "—the messenger angel flew over the manger?"

No one responded at first. Then Scott nodded. "You could put in a track on the beam over the altar. You can't damage the wood, but we could use some strapping hefty enough to hold someone around fifty pounds or so."

"Wait a minute," Tess cut in, once again the voice of reason. "You want to dangle someone's child from the ceiling of the church?"

"Oh, I've got a student who'd do it in a heartbeat," Amy assured her. "He played Peter Pan and said the flying was his favorite part. Scott and Jason did the rigging for us, and it worked perfectly."

After some more back and forth on the basics, Scott and Jason broke off into a huddle with their wives to hash out artistic and engineering logistics. Someone called out Paul's name, so he and Chelsea promised to catch up with Tess later and moved off into the crowd.

Alone for the first time all day, Tess's stomach growled as she eyed the overflowing buffet table. She hadn't eaten since breakfast, and suddenly she was starving.

While she was contemplating where to start, Heath appeared at her side with two full plates and a grin. "Thought you might be hungry."

"Famished." Taking the food from him, she smiled. "How did you know?"

"You were eyeballing the buffet like a half-starved wolf. I took a shot."

He was so cocky about it, she couldn't resist yanking his chain. "Like you did when you asked me to marry you?"

"Sorta." His grin made it clear he knew very well what she was doing and it didn't bother him in the least. "That was more of a timing thing, though."

"Really? So you weren't worried I might say no?" Popping a strawberry in her mouth, she gave him the skeptical look she'd once trotted out on a daily basis but hardly ever used anymore.

"Nah. Even if you did, I'd just ask you again sometime." Slipping his arms around her waist, he reeled her in for a kiss.

"And if I said no again?"

"I'm a pretty patient guy. Eventually I'd wear you down."

"Let me get this straight," she teased, toying with the burgundy tie that to her knowledge was the only one he owned. "You'd keep asking until I said yes, no matter how long it took?"

"Yup."

"Why?"

One of those sunshine grins slowly worked its way across his rugged features, and he leaned in to nuzzle her ear. "Because you're worth the trouble."

"Good answer."

\* \* \* \* \*

Dear Reader,

I love Thanksgiving! It's often overlooked in our eagerness to get to Christmas, but for our family, it's a great time to get everyone together and catch up on what's been happening throughout the year. Not to mention have a great meal and watch football.

Sometimes, when you're looking for something, the hardest part is figuring out where to search. The opportunity that opened up for Tess at Barrett's Sawmill might have seemed nutty at first, but she believed it was at least a step in the right direction. From Heath, she learned how to listen to her heart. His generous, forgiving example encouraged her to put aside her old ways and embrace what's truly important: faith, family and friends.

Heath's experience in Alaska gives him a unique perspective on the future, which for him needs to include a family. He wasn't planning on falling in love with someone as challenging as Tess, but he's smart enough to recognize that the best things in life are worth some extra effort. Fortunately for both of them, they find a way to make things work and end their year looking forward to a long happily-ever-after. It's a reminder to all of us that the past is only part of who we are. The rest is up to us.

If you'd like to stop by for a visit, you'll find me online at www.miaross.com, Facebook, Twitter, and Goodreads. While you're there, send me a message in your favorite format. I'd love to hear from you!

*Mia Ross*

# LARGER-PRINT BOOKS!

**GET 2 FREE
LARGER-PRINT NOVELS
PLUS 2 FREE
MYSTERY GIFTS**

*Love Inspired®*

# SUSPENSE
RIVETING INSPIRATIONAL ROMANCE

## Larger-print novels are now available...